JIM WELLS

JIM WELLS

•

KENT CONWELL

AVALON BOOKS
THOMAS BOUREGY AND COMPANY, INC.
401 LAFAYETTE STREET
NEW YORK, NEW YORK 10003

PRINTED IN THE UNITED STATES OF AMERICA
ON ACID-FREE PAPER
BY HADDON CRAFTSMEN, SCRANTON, PENNSYLVANIA

To Gayle

Chapter One

The plain, unvarnished truth is I am not a thief; I'm not a bank robber; I'm not any kind of outlaw. Now, just because I'm not on the owlhoot trail doesn't necessarily mean I'm smart like a schoolteacher. I'm not. But, I'm not so dumb that rocks bounce around inside my head either, although I'll admit I've done enough moronic stunts to fill the Grand Canyon.

But I reckon the most witless move I ever made was the day I rode into Dallas and pulled up at the hitching rail in front of the Trail's End Saloon. If I'd known I was going to be caught up in a bizarre and insane chase all the way up to Boston Harbor, I would of dug my spurs in my pony and headed for Indian Territory where the only thing I had to worry about was ten thousand savages on the warpath.

But, I didn't know, so there I was, sitting in front of the saloon in the middle of the day. The summer sun was so hot it could blister the ugly off a hog. My

1

throat was parched, my belly growled louder than a squalling cat, and my pockets were emptier than my head. I was just about as rundown a cowpoke as you could ever imagine.

I slouched in my saddle, staring at the cool darkness of the saloon, trying to dredge up some idea to panhandle me a beer and sandwich. Suddenly, a cowpoke reined up beside me. "Hey, pardner. Wanna make a buck?"

For a moment, I was leery. I'd already run into a couple jaspers up on the Red River that took away my dream of a ranch, and I sure didn't need any more trouble. But I was so hungry and thirsty that his question conjured up immediate visions of a pitcher of cold beer and a stack of sandwiches in my sun-feebled brain, blunting my caution. "Who do I have to kill?"

He grinned and flipped me a dollar. "Nobody." He handed me the reins of three saddled ponies. "A friend of mine is down at the bank waiting for these critters. I got business across the street at the meat house. Just tie 'em to the rail."

Well, that seemed sensible to me, but I shoulda figured something was out of kilter. Nobody pays a dollar for a two-minute ride, but my stomach overcame my common sense. I followed his instructions, tied the ponies, then turned back to the saloon.

That's when the gunfire started. Being no one's fool, I leaped from the saddle and tried to dig a hole under the plank sidewalk.

Next thing I knew, half a dozen grim cowpokes were jamming the muzzles of their .45's into my back.

For the next two hours, I sat glued to a hard-backed chair trying to convince an overweight sheriff and his three deputies that I was merely an innocent simpleton and not a hardcase bank robber. But the longer I pleaded, the more stubborn Sheriff Hicks became.

Somewhere around supper time, another cowpoke showed up, a lean, wiry mesquite post wearing bat-wing *chaparreras*. Strange dress for Dallas. *Chaparreras* are generally worn in the brasado country of south and west Texas.

He eyed me curiously, then called the sheriff aside. All I could hear were faint whispers, but I started getting real jittery when they kept throwing sidelong glances at me.

Finally, Sheriff Hicks grunted and gestured to a cell. "Toss Mr. Wells in the first cell, boys. Then get some supper."

I don't know what's worse, being bellowed at or just locked away and forgotten. All I know is that in that cell all by my lonesome, my imagination started working overtime. What did the sheriff have in mind? A trial? Or maybe just a simple lynching?

It wasn't long before I had worked myself up into a real lather.

Ten minutes later, Sheriff Hicks and the cowpoke in chaps came back in. The sheriff set a tray covered with a red-checkered cloth on his desk. The rich smell of beans and hot corn bread set my mouth to watering.

Without a word, he unlocked the cell and nodded to the plate of grub while the other cowpoke poured a cup of coffee for me. I thought I'd died and gone to heaven. It's surprising how all your worries vanish when you plop yourself down in front of hot grub.

The two of them pulled up the ladder-back chairs and straddled them, resting their forearms on the straight backs. They watched silently while I shoveled the grub down my gullet.

While I was eating, a silent figure opened the door and just stood in the shadows. Neither lawman paid him any attention, and all I could make of the new-comer was his shiny eastern shoes and white spats.

Just about the time I was polishing off the beans and sopping up the juice with the last of the corn bread, the sheriff leaned back, patted his watermelon-sized belly and cleared his throat. "I reckon you know you've got a mighty big problem here, Mr. Wells. Aidin' and abettin' a bank robbery."

All those beans turned to stones in my belly. Before I could defend myself, he continued in a patronizing tone. "Now I know what you claim. And, I guess to some, what you say makes sense, but the fact is, you was seen snubbing down the robbers' horses to the hitching rail in front of the bank. Now, intentional or not, that makes you a con . . . a consortin . . ." He frowned and looked at the other cowboy.

"What the sheriff is trying to say is you are a conspirator, an accomplice, Mr. Wells. Subject to the same penalties as those that planned the robbery." That was the first time I'd heard the other cowpoke speak, and from the smoothness in his voice and the way his tongue handled those two-dollar words, I knew he wasn't no grubline-riding cowboy.

"Yep," chimed in Sheriff Hicks almost gleefully. "And Mr. Rozell here will testify that bank robbing here in Dallas usually calls for a necktie party. Us here in Dallas is what you would call *sophistokers* who don't put up with no nonsense."

Rozell rolled his eyes.

Suddenly, I had the strange feeling that something didn't quite fit, just what, I couldn't really put my finger on, but it was that same uncomfortable feeling I got when that old man who raised me threatened "Or else." Like when you hear a boot drop. You wait, almost not breathing, for the other one to hit the floor. And that was the same, exact feeling I had at that moment.

"Look, Sheriff. I told you the truth. What else can I tell you to make you believe me?"

Neither lawman replied. They just stared at me with cold, empty eyes.

With a groan, Sheriff Hicks heaved his ponderous body from the chair and fished a pack of Bull Durham from his pocket. He took his time rolling a cigarette. He popped the match head with his thumbnail, touched the flame to the cigarette, and inhaled deeply. He blew the smoke into the air and watched it drift to the open rafters before he spoke.

"Well, there might be a way me and you can work out our problems, Mr. Wells. Fact is, I reckon I agree that you was nothing more than a . . . " He shrugged and gave me a wry grin. "Well, let's just leave it at they just took advantage of your good and trustin' nature."

For a fleeting moment, my hopes soared, and then Mr. Rozell spoke up. "Just because the sheriff and me might believe you, Mr. Wells, doesn't mean spit. According to the law, you're still guilty. We're duty bound to hold you over for the judge."

"Yeah." Sheriff Hicks grunted. "And old Judge Redstone ain't a forgivin' hombre. Fact is, he could put Isaac Parker to shame when it comes to hanging folks." He flicked the cigarette ashes on the floor.

I grew light-headed and weak-kneed, but Rozell kept me from fainting when he removed his hat and ran his fingers through his short-cut hair. "On the other hand, it could be Judge Redstone might be persuaded to look at some extenuating circumstances."

Sheriff Hicks broke in. "If you're smart, Wells, you best don't let the judge look at anything else. You're already in enough trouble without giving him more ammunition."

Rozell rolled his eyes again. "Not exactly, Sheriff.

Extenuating means some kind of reason to modify the sentence. In other words, if Mr. Wells here does something for the judge, the judge'll do something for him.''

Hicks's face colored. He drew up his shoulders and threw out his chest. ''I knew that.''

''I know you did, Sheriff,'' replied Rozell. ''I know you did.''

Now, like I said before, I'm not the brightest jasper in Texas, but I sure ain't the dumbest. Even a simpleton like me could read between the lines that they wanted to make a deal. What puzzled me was what they figured I had to offer. I looked at the sheriff. He wore an embarrassed grin on his pan-shaped face.

I leaned back in my chair. ''What do you have in mind, Sheriff?''

He gestured to Rozell. ''I reckon Mr. Rozell there had best explain to you. He knows better'n me just what him and his department is looking for.''

Rozell pushed his hat to the back of his head and eyed me steadily. The grin faded from his face. ''You ever heard of the Secret Service, Mr. Wells?''

I glanced at Sheriff Hicks. The cigarette dangled from his fat lips. I looked back to Rozell. Was this some kind of joke? He was solemn-faced, so I figured his question was on the up-and-up. ''New one on me. Is it like the Ku Klux Klan? I'm not much on joining secret clubs and such.''

''It's not a club we're asking you to join, Mr. Wells. We want you for a spy!''

Chapter Two

A spy!

My reply choked in my throat. I banged the heel of my hand against the side of my head, wondering if I'd heard the man right. Finally, I managed to croak. "A spy? You want me to be a spy?"

The sheriff grinned, but the lean cowpoke's face remained impassive. "For the Secret Service, Mr. Wells. It's a department of the United States government." He fished out his wallet and flipped it open, revealing a shiny badge. "I'm a Special Agent for the Secret Service. Our organization was established thirteen years ago in 1865 to curtail counterfeiting, which is becoming a major problem today, especially since the greenback will be convertible to gold next year."

"So what? That doesn't mean anything to me."

"It does to the government. You see, presently, greenbacks are not convertible to gold. That is, you can't swap them for gold whenever you want to. At

7

one time, they were to be discontinued, but the Grange and its lobbyists in Washington gave them new life. Because they were never intended to be the currency of the land, the printing process. . . . '' He hesitated at the frown on my face. ''Do you understand what I'm talking about, Mr. Wells?''

I understood most of the words. It was the way they were all put together that confused me. ''Not exactly. I'd sooner have things explained nice and simple.''

He grinned. ''Me too. Here it is then, nice and simple. The greenbacks in circulation today are easy to copy. The counterfeiters print them and sell them at a discount to connections back East. We want to stop the scheme before it goes any farther.''

''Okay. I understand that, but . . . I . . . '' I stammered and stuttered, making no sense at all. Finally, I managed to sputter out a protest. ''I'm no spy. I'm not sure I really know what spies do.''

Sheriff Hicks's grin broadened. ''Not yet you ain't no spy, but you will be.'' The tip of the cigarette bounced up and down as he spoke.

I stared at the sheriff, not really understanding his words. Then it hit me. I eyed each of them skeptically. They had me backed into a corner. As neat as a hideskinner pops the skin off a buffalo. Sheriff Hicks wore a smug grin. Rozell just stared at me, his face inscrutable like one of those China boys.

These two were moving mighty fast. I figured I might as well slow them down a bit. ''Well, now, Mr. Rozell. You might figure you got me hog-tied, but I've seen many a critter kick loose of the piggins just when I thought I had him ready for the iron.''

A faint smile broke the stony expression on his face. ''Could be, Mr. Wells, but in your case, I don't think so. Besides, you carry out the job we give you, and you're two thousand dollars richer and a free man.''

Two thousand! I stared at him, my jaw hanging open.

Suddenly, the figure in the shadows by the door muttered. Rozell stepped to his side and listened. I saw the lawman's head nod, then he came back into the lamplight. ''Make it five thousand.''

Five thousand! If my jaw could have dropped any more, it would have bounced off the floor. I babbled a couple times, making no sense at all.

''You heard me right, Mr. Wells. Five thousand. Five thousand dollars in sound American gold, not greenbacks. A sizeable enough grubstake to set you up with a small ranch of your own.''

Now, I'd be lying if I said his offer didn't make me take a look at the situation from a whole different angle. Strange how money can do that, especially if you don't have any. But, I didn't want to rush into anything. I wanted to approach the entire setup cautiously. ''I don't cotton to any killing. A little innocent robbery maybe, or rustling, or kidnapping, but no killing.''

Rozell shook his head. ''None of that, Mr. Wells. All you have to do is dig up some information for us.''

Sheriff Hicks ground the cigarette butt under his heel and nodded. The Secret Service man fished a folded sheet of paper from his vest and handed it to me.

I opened the paper and gaped. It was a wanted poster. Despite the grainy texture, the picture was like looking into a mirror. The same angular face with the high cheekbones. The same pug nose. The same lantern chin. Even the same color hair, except his was curly, and mine was straight as the barrel of my Winchester.

Phillip Rozell spoke. ''Name's Walter Caruthers. Goes by Curly. Right now he's doing twenty years in Huntsville. He's been hired by the Weems gang down in Bandera. That's the gang we suspect of the counterfeiting. We're not sure they're mixed up in it, but that's what we want to find out. Your mission is to find out if they are involved in a counterfeiting scheme. Since you two look enough alike to be twins, we want you to join up with them, learn their plans, and then get word back to us. If they are mixed up in the scheme, set them up so we can nail their hides to the fence, and you're out of this mess free and clear with five thousand dollars stuck in your hip pocket.''

I studied Rozell for several seconds. What he was asking was risky, mighty risky. ''Can I have some time to think about it?'' Such a decision shouldn't be made too quickly.

''Sure,'' he replied. ''No problem. You got two minutes.'' He gave me a smug grin.

At that moment, I would have been mighty pleased to try to stomp his cocksure carcass into the ground. But, this round, he was the dealer. Still, I didn't want him to think he got me too easy. Although I already knew the answer, I asked him another question, figuring it might irritate him a little. ''What if I say no?''

He shrugged. ''We'll just wait for Judge Redstone.''

A wry grin curled my lips despite my effort to stop it. ''You don't give a jasper much of a chance, do you?''

Rozell returned my grin. ''Not much.''

Behind him, Sheriff Hicks chuckled.

I drew a deep breath and slowly released it. Maybe if I asked enough questions, I could punch some holes in his plan. "Well, Mr. Rozell. Looks like you're holding all the cards. One question though. What if the gang finds out this Caruthers jasper's still in jail?"

"They won't. We've already moved him out. He's under heavy guard up at Fort Sill."

So much for that question, so I came up with another. "You say we look enough alike to be twins. What about the hair? His is curly. Mine's straight." I resisted a smug smile. I had him on this one.

"No problem. We'll give you some new-fangled thing called a curl."

I looked at him suspiciously. "What's that?"

He wiggled his fingers in his hair. "One of our agents just returned from India with a special salve that will hold your hair in any position you want. We're going to get a lady to fix your hair in curls, then soak it down with that salve. It'll be a little greasy, but that won't hurt nothing. I don't know exactly how it's all done, but we'll get it figured out before we do it to you."

Hicks started snickering.

I stared at Rozell in shock. I would have sooner sold my saddle than have some woman fixing my hair in kinky little curls. I backed away. "No. Forget it. Not me, not that."

Phillip Rozell arched an eyebrow. "There's always Judge Redstone."

Sheriff Hicks laughed out loud.

The look I gave him would have straightened a horseshoe. I turned back to the Secret Service man. I was almost pleading. "Just shave my head. I can tell them I had head lice or something."

"Nope. It's the curls or Redstone."

I couldn't reply. He had me good and proper, between the rock and the hard place.

After a few moments, he took my silence as tacit

approval. "Don't worry, Mr. Wells." He nodded to the gathering darkness outside. "We've got as much reason keeping this quiet as you do. We'll bring the hair lady in after dark, so no one will know what we're up to. While she's working on your hair, I'll fill you in on the gang members. There's a few things you'll need to know."

Rozell stepped in front of me, and that's when the shadowy figure opened the door and stepped outside. I tried to peer around Rozell, but all I saw was the retreating back of the unknown jasper who had added three thousand dollars to my pot.

Well, sir, I'm not even going to dignify the hair-curling episode by talking about it. It's enough to say it took place, and that I tried to ignore it by paying close attention to Agent Rozell's explanation of what I was expected to do, which turned out to be another mistake. The more he talked, the less I liked it, and the more determined I was to find a back door I could slip out.

The Weems gang was made up of three bothers with lengthy records. More than a dozen unsolved murders had been attributed to the gang. "We can't prove it, one way or the other, but I don't really believe they're killers," Rozell added. "From what little we know about the brothers, they're just two-bit outlaws who are trying to step up a notch."

"Where does Caruthers fit in?" I asked while the hairdresser was rolling a strip of my hair in a circle and sticking some kind of pin on it. I tried not to watch, pretending nothing so degrading was happening to me.

Phillip Rozell paused to roll a Durham. "The way we understand it, Weems met Caruthers in Fort Worth when he hired him. Caruthers was supposed to have some connections back East. The next morning, we arrested Caruthers. We figure they only spent a few hours together.''

''You figure? What if you're wrong? That could get me killed.''

Rozell shrugged. ''For your sake then, we'd better not be wrong.''

I groaned and shook my head. The hairdresser scolded me. ''You've got to be still if you want this to turn out right.''

I resisted the urge to tell her my true feelings. ''Sorry.'' I held my head motionless and looked at Rozell from the corner of my eyes. I tried another angle. ''What if one of the Weems brings up something that took place that night? How in the Sam Hill do I handle that?''

''Easy. Tell him you got drunk later that night, and you can't remember a thing that happened.''

''What if he doesn't buy that?'' I was skeptical. His answer was too simple.

Rozell paused to take a drag off his cigarette and expel the smoke. ''He will. We arrested Curly when he was leaving Madam Kate's, and according to Kate, Curly was the only one there that night.'' A faint smile cracked the sober expression on his face.

I searched for some other excuse. ''How long do these curls last? What happens when they grow out? Won't the gang figure something's wrong?''

Rozell's grin broadened. ''We don't know how long the curls last. This curling business is brand-spanking new. The one thing we know for certain is that you can't wash your hair.''

''What?'' I touched my fingers to my greasy curls. ''I got enough grease on my head to fry a dozen steaks. I need to get some of it off.''

He shook his head. ''Don't do it. The story we got

from our agent in India was that this salve is used in some kind of ritual that calls for bald heads. They put it on their heads and fashion their hair in all kinds of foolish styles. Then they wait until the monsoons hit and dance in the rain until they go bald. That's the one characteristic of this salve that we can't explain. We don't know why, but if you wash your hair, it'll all fall out, right then. You can't even let the rain hit it.''

I stared at him in goggle-eyed disbelief. When I found my voice, I managed to choke out my next question, a sensible, intelligent question. ''What the blazes do you mean, it'll fall out?''

''Just what I said. It'll fall out. Your head will be slick as the seat of your saddle. Now, I'm not saying not to wash it, but if I was you, I'd wait until I contacted the Weems brothers and got myself accepted as Curly Caruthers.''

He paused and rolled a cigarette. ''Personally, I'd leave it alone until the whole business was over. You turn up bald one morning, they might ask a bunch of questions. The sensible thing would be to work fast and get us the information before anything happens.''

Before I could reply, the hairdresser stepped in front of me, cocked her head, and studied her handiwork. ''That looks just dandy,'' she said with a big smile. ''Just dandy.'' She glanced at Phillip Rozell. ''You know, I imagine there are a lot of women out there who would love to have beautiful curls like this.'' She paused. Her forehead knit in thoughtfulness. ''If you can just figure out some way to keep the hair from falling out.''

All I could do was groan. The need to blister the walls with wild profanity tugged at my willpower, but there was a lady present. I was sunk. With a deep sigh, I resigned myself to whatever lay ahead.

"Good," I said with a grunt. "I'm glad somebody's happy."

When I looked in the mirror, I thought I was going to be sick. I looked like a black sheep. My hair curled tighter than an angry rattlesnake, and shiny as the seat of worn-out pants.

Rozell didn't give me time to feel sorry for myself. He tossed me my gunbelt and wallet, which had been packed with greenbacks. "Your pony's down at O'Keefe's Livery. Don't waste time. Your contact works in the Empty Bucket Saloon in Bandera. That's your line of communication to me."

"What if I decide to just ride out? Leave the territory?" I pulled my gunbelt tight around my waist. "How would you stop me?"

Rozell arched an eyebrow. "Couldn't. Of course, you'd be on the run for the rest of your life." His voice grew menacing. "And when you were caught— and you would be sooner or later—I'd make sure you stretched a rope from the nearest tree."

Our eyes locked for several moments. I could have happily blown his head off, but he was right. I had tossed my lasso on a wild longhorn, and I couldn't let go. "This contact. What's his name?"

"Don't worry. You'll be contacted."

"Who by? Can't you tell me that?"

"Not really. I'm not sure who we got there. The last agent was buried a couple weeks ago. I haven't met the new one."

I stared at him. Danged if every time that man opened his mouth I didn't find myself deeper in trouble.

He nodded to the door. "You're burning daylight." He glanced out the window. "I mean, burning night-time. Good luck, Curly."

Anxious to reach the rolling prairie to the southwest, I picked up my pony and headed down the dusty street, which was lit by street lamps. I was still toying with the idea of lighting a shuck out of the state. There was always California. I'd heard talk about the San Joaquin Valley around a place called Los Angeles.

Shouting voices interrupted my musings. I ignored them, knowing they couldn't be directed at me. They persisted, and I glanced around to see what was causing such a commotion. Two men were standing in the middle of the street, their hands filled with six-guns, and they were staring at me.

One of the hombres shouted. "Curly! Curly Caruthers! Slap leather, or I'll shoot you down like a mangy dog."

I had been so absorbed in considering California that it still hadn't dawned on me just who those two jaspers was figuring on planting in a pine box. I looked over my shoulder to see who the unfortunate soul was. There was no one behind me. Suddenly, like the kick of a mule, I realized they were talking to me!

In the next instant, two shots rang out. One slug burned my shoulder, and the other took off my hat. Without hesitation, I dug my spurs into my cow pony and charged the two gunslingers, unleathering my own six-gun at the same time.

I ran over the one on the left and slapped the barrel of my handgun across the other one's temple. Wheeling the pony about, I stomped over them again and then quickly dismounted and kicked their six-guns away.

Five minutes later, I was back in the jail, sticking my nose into Phillip Rozell's face. "Forget it. Bushwhacking wasn't included in this deal."

His tone was soft and cold. "Old Curly has made a heap of enemies. I reckon you better keep one eye on the front and the other on the back. That is, if you still want to go through with it. If you don't, yonder's your cell.''

The sight of the jail cell cooled me off mighty fast. I really didn't have much of a choice. Either I stay in jail and get hung, or I ride out to Bandera and get shot. Some choice. Well, at least Rozell's way, I'd have a chance to see some more of the country before some bushwhacker jumped out from behind a tree and back-shot me.

So once again I rode out, but this time I kept a close eye on every single citizen walking the streets. I'd got lucky with those first two, but the only thing certain about luck was that sooner or later, it'll damn well change.

Chapter Three

Every night I pitched camp, I swore that the next morning I was going to cut and run. But every morning, I saddled up and continued southwest.

The old man who raised me down in Jim Wells County always taught me that the most important thing in a man's life was for him to feel good about himself. Now, that might seem strange coming from a gambler, but Larimer H. Harrison played the game with pride and self-respect.

So, I couldn't run. I'd been neatly shanghaied, and there was no way out except straight ahead.

The fifth day, I pulled out of Round Rock and headed for the Colorado River. Beyond the Colorado, the country grew rougher, bluffs of gray limestone looking over vast carpets of thick scrub oak and red berry juniper, the lush growth watered by clear streams of sweet water.

About the only problem I had with my hair was

that I had to keep my hat on, even when I slept. The grease wasn't too bad, but it drew bugs, all manner of bugs. I discovered that little distraction the first night out of Dallas when I woke up and discovered a passel of june bugs was having a square dance in my hair.

At Fredericksburg, I hit the narrow, twisting road to Bandera, a hard day's ride ahead. That night, I camped in a copse of live oak on the back side of a hill overlooking the small village.

I slept but little, too fidgety, too worried about what the coming day would try to shove in my face. Abruptly, I sat up and stared into the dark night. "Hold it right there, Jim Wells," I said aloud to myself. "You been grumbling worse'n any trail drive cookie I've known. It's time to stop cryin' and get on with what you got to do."

The chirruping crickets and singing birds must've heard me talking to myself like a crazy man for the night grew quiet as a stalking cat.

After all, it wasn't like in the olden days when those Roman fellers threw them Christians to the lions. I could fight. I was right handy with a six-gun and Winchester. And my bony knuckles had enough scars that I had no reason to hang my head.

No, the only part of the whole deal that spooked me was the fact that I had no idea what was going to happen, what they would say, who I would meet. Now, that's not so bad if a man's just being himself, but when he's trying to pass himself off as another— well, it isn't the same. I had to keep my guard up every minute. Not one second would pass that I could relax.

Lying back on my blanket, I stared at the stars shining like the lights of a bright city, remembering that

Rozell had insisted Caruthers and Weems had never met until that time in Fort Worth.

"So," I muttered to the stars. "It won't be like Caruthers was going back to a welcome home party. He'll be as much the stranger there as I would be." And from now on, I reminded myself, I'm Curly Caruthers. Get used to that name, and forget that you ever answered to the handle, Jim Wells.

I grinned at the stars and pulled the blanket up under my chin. Now, I could sleep. Even the yipping of the prowling coyotes or squalling mountain lions couldn't keep me awake.

I reined up on the outskirts of town and took a deep breath. Now, I had to find my contact, or he had to find me. Either way, I needed to know who were my friends and who were my enemies. The only certainty was that when I found out, the enemies were bound to outweigh the friends.

I rode into town with every sense alert. I had pulled the brim of my hat low over my eyes so the shadows would hide them while they scoured the town for any danger.

Bandera was a rundown collection of clapboard and canvas buildings leaning in every direction like a company of drunken soldiers, the largest being the Empty Bucket Saloon. Across the rocky street was a second saloon, smaller, dirtier, sporting a battered sign that merely read "Beer." Two dry goods stores, a hotel, a blacksmith shop, and naturally, a lawyer's office completed the town.

Two ponies were hitched in front of the blacksmith shop, and the still morning air rang with the clanging of the blacksmith's hammer against the anvil. The blacksmith paused when I rode by. He and a lean cowpoke stared at me curiously. One old man sat in a rickety chair in front of Edwards's Dry Goods, whittling away. Like the other two, he stared at me. I ignored all three and headed directly for the Empty Bucket, the saloon always being the first place a parched cowboy visited in a new town.

I pulled up at the hitching rail and sat motionless for several seconds. Then, so no one watching would miss my curls, I deliberately removed my hat and ran my fingers through my spanking new curly hair. I shivered all the way down my spine when I felt those greasy kinks.

Dismounting, I looped the reins around the hitching rail and took my time entering the saloon, intentionally pausing at the batwing doors and studying the town. A buckboard rattled down the street, driven by a hefty young woman wearing men's clothes. Her bright red hair stuck out in all directions from under her hat. She glanced at me, then did a double take, keeping her eyes on me until she passed.

I shrugged and glanced at my dirt-stained clothes. I could use a good cleaning up. Behind me, the tinny sounds of a piano floated out the door, inviting me inside. First things first.

I bellied up to the bar and ordered a shot of whiskey and a mug of beer. The whiskey was rank, and the beer was warm, but they had the sweetest taste I could remember. Chugging the beer, I ordered another. "What kinda grub you got, barkeep?" I pushed my hat to the back of my head, exposing my curls for all to see.

The bartender was a short, slender man with a ready grin and a cheery voice. He drew my beer. "Nothing hot, stranger. Just meat and cheese and bread. You want a plate?"

I studied him a moment. Was he my contact?

"Yeah." I took the beer. "I'll be back at the rear table."

From the rear table, I looked the saloon over. Three cowpokes sat at a table playing poker. One old man sat by the door nursing a half-full mug of beer. Across the room, the piano backed up to a flight of stairs leading to the second floor. A brightly painted saloon girl leaned against the piano, a mug of beer in her hand and tears in her eyes as the piano player banged out his version of "Sweet Betsy from Pike."

The little barkeep brought a plate heaped with beef, cheese, and bread, all fresh and sliced thick. "Here you go, stranger. Two bits."

I flipped him a coin, and he caught it in midair. Without a hitch in his cheery voice and a flicker of his smile, he asked, "You happen to be Mr. Caruthers?"

Without hesitation, I reached for the bread and started building a sandwich. "Why?" I replied, keeping my eyes on the plate.

"No offense, mister. I been paid to ask ever' stranger who comes through here. If you be this Caruthers gent, you ride out the south road, cross the creek, and about three miles down, take the left fork. The gentleman who hired you lives there. If you ain't him, please accept my apologies for bothering you."

By this time, the sandwich was four inches thick. Holding it in both hands, I hesitated before taking a bite. "You got the wrong hombre, barkeep, but I wouldn't mind a job. My *dinero* is just about gone. Could be I'll stop in on this feller and see if he could use another hand."

The barkeep shrugged. "George Weems has got about seven or eight hired hands. Could be he might use another."

I studied the bartender as he returned to the bar.

Was he the contact? He'd made no effort to identify himself. Maybe it was because I didn't admit to being Caruthers. I looked over the other jaspers in the saloon.

One of the cowpokes at the poker table saw me staring at them. He had a dark birthmark on his cheek. He nodded to the table. "Want to sit in, stranger?"

"Thanks." I shook my head. "I'm just about busted now. No sense in handing over what little I got to you gents."

Something tugged at my arm. I looked around and the old man stood beside me. "Buy me a beer, stranger?" He was bleary-eyed and unshaven. He smelled gamy as a week-dead buffalo.

Some folks said that was one of my weaknesses, doling out money to panhandlers and tramps. I never looked at it like that. I just figured it to be a hedge against the time I might be in their boots.

I turned back to the bartender and nodded. He reached for a clean mug for the old man.

"Here you go, Sam," he said.

Sam looked down at me, embarrassed. He tried to grin.

"Forget it," I said.

With a gleeful nod, he shuffled over to the bar. Well, I could mark him off as a contact.

A few minutes later, the poker game broke up. On the way out, the cowpoke with the birthmark stopped at my table. The other two pulled up beside him. "Don't mean to butt in, Mister, but I couldn't help overhearing you and Willy, the bartender. If you're really looking for work, about ten miles out is the Chapman spread. Mr. Chapman, he's an honest man."

I arched an eyebrow. "You saying Weems isn't?"

"Nope. Just saying that Chapman is a good man to work for. You hang around awhile, and you'll learn what I mean.'' He grinned, touched his fingers to the brim of his hat, and the three walked out into the morning sunlight.

"Don't pay any attention to Patches," a voice at my side said.

I looked up into the painted face of the saloon girl.

Without asking, she slid into the chair next to me and waved to Willy. Her gaze lit on my greasy curls, then slipped on down to my eyes. "Patches sometimes lets his imagination run away from him."

"Patches?" I looked around at the cowboy just as he pushed through the batwing doors.

"Yeah. That feller with the mark on his face. That's what we call him, Patches." I looked back at her and frowned. "He used to work for Charlie Weems, but he quit. Never said why. Most of us figure him and Charlie got into it, and Charlie came out on top."

Willy, the bartender, slid a mug of beer on the table before the girl. "That's a dime," he said, looking at me.

I paid him, glad to get the chance to question her for such a small price. "Who is this Weems hombre? Seems like he's caused some strong feelings around here."

She shrugged. "Just a rancher. Like all of them. What he's done, ever' rancher's done at one time or the other."

"You mean like mavericking or slick-earing."

She smiled, and for a saloon girl, that smile was right becoming. That's when I noticed her hair was a natural looking blond. "Something like that." She turned up her beer and gulped half of it down. "My name's Lucy, Cowboy. What's yours?"

Before I could reply, several more customers pushed through the door. Lucy grinned sheepishly and rose. "Business before pleasure. Come back to see us, Cowboy." She arched an eyebrow. "We're good company around here."

I watched her leave. What a life, I thought to myself. Has to be tough to make a living like that. Then again, I reminded myself, look what I'm doing.

Leaning back in my chair and rubbing my full stomach, I noticed a small slip of paper under the plate. With a frown, I opened it and froze. Quickly, I looked around the saloon. No one was watching me. I read the note again. *Tonight. Ten o'clock. Behind the blacksmith.*

Casually, I slipped the note in my vest pocket. Who left it? The bartender, the old man? Maybe one of the three cowpokes, or could it have been the girl, Lucy? Whoever did it was slicker than bear fat.

Rising, I headed for the door. At least I'd made contact. My only problem was that I didn't know with who.

Chapter Four

Ignoring the curious stares thrown my way, I rode out of town on the south road, heading for the Weems' place. The noonday sun beat down, a white, blistering orb in the washed-out sky.

After discovering the note, I considered hanging around until the next morning, but decided against the idea. No sense Weems wondering just why I laid over in town. And no sense in taking chances with someone else reading the note. I tore it into pieces and scattered it along the road.

At the creek, I filled my canteen and watered my pony. I stared at the cool water wistfully, then ran a rag through my hair to remove some grease. Seemed like that grease just made more grease, like rabbits.

I glanced to the west. Wild country, I could lose myself for years, maybe forever. I resisted the urge to run. I was nervous. No, not nervous, but scared. I was so scared my stomach was doing flip-flops, and the closer I got to the Weems Ranch, the more spooked I became.

"Get hold of yourself," I muttered, clenching my teeth and climbing into the saddle. "Those jaspers don't know you from John Brown. All you got to do is remember that your name is . . . " I froze. My name! What the blazes was my name? I racked my brain and sighed with relief as I remembered. "That's it. Curly . . . Curly Caruthers."

I rode on toward the ranch. If I thought I had been antsy before, now I was as skittish as a three-tailed cat in a roomful of rocking chairs. I closed my eyes and tried to pull up the picture of George Weems that Rozell had shown me. I had to recognize him immediately.

The San Antone road wound over and around the rugged gray bluffs until it opened onto a wide, open plain. Immediately, the road forked, and I angled down the left one, which wound around the base of a sheer granite bluff pillared with great stone columns.

Nestled back in the sweeping canyon was the Weems Ranch. I clicked my tongue and flipped the leather thong off the hammer of my six-gun as my pony broke into a trot. I had entered the gates of harm's way.

Great orange and gray longhorns as well as smaller mixed breeds grazed across the savanna. Beyond the ranch house, a herd of blooded Kentucky thoroughbreds fed. It was a decent looking spread, not one where you would expect to find a band of outlaws holed up.

The ranch house was board and batten, weathered gray. The portico covering the porch had several planks missing, permitting rectangular patches of sunlight to fall on the porch. Nobody had bothered to maintain the place.

I pulled up at the rail and started to dismount.

"Hold it, cowboy."

My leg froze half hiked over the saddle. I looked at the sound of the voice and stared into the muzzle of a .45.

"You ain't been invited to light."

I looked up into the face of a smirking redhead with a flat nose, like it had been busted five or six times. I just grinned and climbed back into the saddle. "Sorry, pardner. You're mighty right. I forgot my manners. Damned improper of me." I shoved my hat back. A couple curls fell across my forehead, and a trickle of grease ran down my nose. I wiped it away.

His grin grew broader, running all his freckles together in one red blotch. "Look what we got us here, Lorenzo," he said to the cowboy who clomped out on the porch, a smaller version of the redhead.

Lorenzo grinned, and his eyes lit up with a vacuous gleam. "Goody. What we goin' to do with him, huh, Albert, huh?" He giggled. "Have some fun, huh?"

Goody? What kind of lingo was that? I blinked my eyes and looked closer at Lorenzo. His eyes glittered as he giggled and glanced at Albert. I had the distinct feeling this one was a couple pickles shy of a barrelful.

Albert tipped the brim of his hat back with the muzzle of his .45. "Don't know about that, Lorenzo. It's been a spell since we had us some fun."

Suddenly a large body burst from the door, slammed Lorenzo aside and sent him tumbling on the porch. The man grabbed Albert and spun him around, driving a crushing right cross into the side of the man's head. "You bovine-brained, pig-headed. . . . " He grunted as his fist bounced off Albert's skull.

Arms outspread, Albert stumbled backward from the blow, struggling to catch his balance. The back of his legs struck the porch rail, and he somersaulted head over heels onto the hardpan. He lay still.

I didn't know if the big man had killed him or what, but one thing I tucked back in my brain was that here was one hombre I never wanted to back into a corner.

He looked up at me, his face twisted in anger. I tensed my muscles. My fingers hung inches from the butt of my six-gun. From the description I had been given, this was George Weems.

Abruptly, the anger vanished from his face, replaced with a broad grin. "Sorry about the greeting, Curly. Climb down and have a drink."

I played the scene cool and collected. "Howdy, George." I nodded to his brothers. "Glad you was around. I didn't want to hurt those boys."

He laughed and gestured to the door. "They ain't bad, just kinda dumb." With that, he kicked the younger brother in the flank. "Get off your tail, Lorenzo, and put Curly's horse in the barn."

"Yeah, boy," I drawled, asserting the arrogance that was as much a part of Caruthers as his curly hair. "And make sure you rub him down good."

George chuckled again and motioned me inside. I led the way, rolling my eyes and breathing deeply. I was past the first hitch. George Weems had accepted me, so far.

I plopped down at the trestle table by the potbellied stove while George set two tin cups on the table and filled them half full of coffee. He reached up in a cabinet and retrieved a bottle of Yellowstone Whiskey, with which he topped off our cups.

"There you go, Curly." He held his cup in a toast. "Here's to all we dreamed about." His gaze flickered to my shiny curls.

I gulped. Dreamed about? Had we talked about something? Had Curly and George talked about something in Dallas, made some kind of definite plans? I touched my cup to his. ''You bet, George.''

He sipped his coffee. His tone took on a trace of wariness. ''Kinda surprised to see you, Curly. I heard they stuck you in jail.''

I sensed his suspicion. ''Yeah. That they did. Next morning after we met. I was coming out of Kate's.'' I took a drink from my cup while I tried to remember my story. ''Sent me to Dallas, but after a couple days, I busted out. Headed west to Fort Griffin, and then cut due south to Fredericksburg. Lost the posse the second day out.''

I glanced at him casually, which was hard to do when you're trying to study a jasper to see if he believes you. Spend too much time staring at him, and he'll begin to wonder. I closed my eyes and licked my lips. ''Mighty good whiskey, George.''

''You must be a lucky gent.'' The grin on his square face was frozen. ''Mighty lucky to escape from one of them prison wagons.''

''Wasn't no prison wagon I escaped from. I told you, it was the jail there in Dallas.'' I sipped from my cup slowly.

George relaxed. ''Oh, yeah. Well, I still say you was mighty lucky.''

''That's one thing old Curly Caruthers has always had an abundance of, George. Luck.''

He frowned like a schoolboy. ''A whut of luck?''

For a moment, he had me confused, then I realized what he meant. ''A lot of luck, George. That's what I meant. I have a lot of luck.''

He thought a moment, then nodded. ''That's what I thought you meant.''

Taking a quick sip of whiskey, I made a mental note to speak only in one syllable words from then on. I didn't want to confuse George.

He nodded at my hair. "What's that on your hair? I don't remember it being that shiny up in Fort Worth."

"The sun," I replied quickly, wondering just what I was going to say next. The words just tumbled out. "That's all I can figure. Seems like all I been doing is sweatin' oil lately." I grinned and added. "One of these days, I reckon I'll have to take a bath. Why even Kate said I needed one."

We both laughed.

"By the way," he added, leaning forward and lowering his voice. "If I was you, I wouldn't mention going to Kate's when Miranda gets back."

Miranda? Inwardly I groaned. Now what had I stepped in? Who was Miranda? "Yeah, I see what you mean."

He grinned, and I grinned back, like two possums, neither knowing what the other one was talking about. "She can be a mite jealous."

The door opened and Albert stomped in followed by Lorenzo. "What for you go knocking me about, George?" demanded Albert in an injured voice. He glanced at me briefly.

George nodded to me. "This here's Curly Caruthers. He's come to help us out with our plan. You best be satisfied I stopped you. This man's mean clear through."

The two younger brothers stared at me, Albert with a challenge in his eye and Lorenzo with his mouth open. That the brothers came from the same pod was evident. Wild mops of red hair, freckles solid on square faces, thick necks so short that their heads seemed to spring out of their broad shoulders.

At first glance, I'd have bet money that George's shoulders were as wide as an axe handle, but after I studied him a few minutes, I realized I was wrong. Two axe handles was a better guess.

Albert turned back to George. "Well, I wasn't going to hurt him. You didn't have to knock me around, George." He laid his fingers against his head. "You gave me a headache now."

George shoved the bottle of whiskey across the table and laughed. "Take a swig, then. That'll make you feel better."

He grinned at me, then grew serious. "Now, Curly, before we talk business, let me set something straight. The boys and me got us a reputation for killers and outlaws. Now, the outlaw business is one thing. We deserve that 'cause we worked hard to be honest outlaws, but we ain't killers. I ain't saying some old boy might not've run into a tree limb and fell off his cayuse chasing us and croaked, but we've never gone out and shot no one deliberate."

I wasn't sure where his explanation was taking us, so I just gave him rein and let him go. "Okay. So, why you tellin' me all this?"

George dropped his gaze to the tabletop and cleared his throat. "I just don't want no intentional killing. That's all." He lifted his gaze to my eyes. "We're only robbers and crooks. On the up-and-up. Just honest robbers and crooks. If that's okay with you, then let's talk business."

"Fine with me, George." I paused and tried to look embarrassed. "But, I reckon, you'll have to do most of the talking. You see, after I left you that night, I got purty drunk, and to be honest, I barely remembered that you'd hired me."

For several tense moments, he stared at me. Then, a wide grin split his face, running his freckles together in blotches. He laughed uproariously until tears rolled down his cheeks. His laughter was catching, for Albert and Lorenzo joined in even though they didn't know what he was laughing about.

When he finally caught his breath, he gasped. "With these brothers of mine here, I've heard my share of wild stories, but that takes the prize. You breaking out of jail and riding down here when you didn't even remember what we'd talked about." He broke into another spasm of laughter.

I grinned and nodded agreeably. I sure didn't see anything funny, but if it made George happy, that was fine with me. Let him laugh all day long if he wanted to.

He wiped the tears from his eyes, trying to subdue the laughter. Just as he took a big gulp of whiskey, he started laughing again and choked himself on the whiskey. That set off Albert and Lorenzo. They laughed and pointed at their big brother.

"Why, you coulda got hitched up with Miranda and never knowed it," he choked out, and all three brothers broke into another round of wheezing and gasping laughter.

I just sat there like I had good sense and grinned and nodded with them. I had fallen in with crazies. But I was just as bad. Here I was, trying to figure out who this Miranda woman was, and now George is talking about her and me getting hitched.

Finally, George calmed down. He motioned to the empty spaces at the table, and the two brothers sat down. "Well, now, Mr. Caruthers. Seeing as you don't remember much of our conversation . . . " He hesitated while he suppressed a snicker. "I could take advantage of you, but you're too valuable to us." He grew serious. "I hired you for your contacts back East."

He rose from the table. "Let me show you something."

In the next room was a small printing press on a table. In one corner of the room were stacks of paper and cans of ink. He picked up a greenback from the table. "Take a look."

The twenty dollar bill was nice and crisp. I gave it a cursory glance. "Looks good to me."

George stuck out his chest and grinned. "That's the kind of work we do. Good work. It's hard to tell it from a real twenty. But, we can only spread the bills just so far around here before folks start getting suspicious. We're a cattle ranch, and there's only so many cattle we can sell. We start throwing money around, and people will begin to wonder where it all came from. That's where you come in. You got connections back East. I figure we can print up five hundred thousand. We'll sell it for twenty-five cents to the dollar."

I arched an eyebrow. "Not bad," I muttered, inspecting the bill closer. I couldn't see any glaring mistakes like a longhorn instead of a buffalo or the wrong color ink. Of course, I was no expert. I pulled a twenty from my pocket and spread it on the table beside the bogus bill for comparison. Not bad, I told myself, studying the bills carefully.

Suddenly, I froze. I blinked my eyes and stared at the bogus bill. Then I glanced at George. "You already printed some of these, George?"

All three brothers grinned proudly. "Twenty thousand dollars so far. We've just been waiting for you to make your contacts before we go whole hog."

I nodded and gazed at the bill on the table, suppressing the full-bellied laughter building up inside. "Yessir," I said, biting the inside of my lip to contain my mirth. "These look mighty good."

Special Agent Phillip Rozell would have no trouble recognizing these bills. Right across the top were the words, *United States of Amurica.*

Chapter Five

I did some fast thinking. Should I point out the mistake or not? Rozell only wanted me to get information that would convict them. And I already had it. The printing press and the bills. All I had to do now was pass the word to my contact at the Empty Bucket, and I had my freedom and five thousand dollars.

But I had to play my cards close to the vest. I'd seen too many jaspers with a winning hand relax and get himself snookered by a smarter player.

I glanced up at the boys and grinned. George was staring at the bogus bill like a proud papa, but Albert just glared at me, still blaming me for George knocking him around, I guess. He didn't trust me. I could see it in his eyes. That meant that wherever I went, he would probably follow, even into Bandera tonight.

So, I did what any good criminal would do. I tossed a monkey wrench in their plans. "Yep, George, the bills look good, but you made a tiny, tiny mistake."

The room was suddenly charged with tension.

George's jaw dropped open. Then his eyes grew cold and his jaw hard. "What the blazes are you talking about, mistake? There ain't no mistake in them bills."

Keeping my voice soft and level, I replied. "Look, boys, we could all end up in federal prison if anything goes wrong with this plan of yours. I've been there. It's no hotel." I handed the bill to George. "You need to learn to spell. America is spelled with an 'e', not a 'u'. It's America, not Amurica."

George's jaw dropped open again. Then his eyes got cold again and his jaw got hard again, but this time, he was glaring at Albert who was still trying to figure out what we were talking about.

George exploded. "You slack-jawed idiot! You said you checked all the writing. You said it was okay."

Albert shot me a dagger look before defending himself to his enraged brother. "It *is* okay." He grew belligerent. "Look, George, I got through the third grade. Miz Pincy taught me how to spell. If I say the writing is okay, it's okay. Miranda even said it was good." He glared at me. "You saying Miz Pincy ain't a good teacher? Why, I oughta whop you upside the head for that. Nobody never talks about my teacher."

"Just calm down, Albert," I said in what I hoped was a soothing tone. "I'm sure Miss Pincy was a fine teacher. I reckon the problem was that the proper spelling of *America* is taught in the fourth grade, not the third. The third is where she taught you to spell *United States*, and you did a good job of that."

That calmed him somewhat, but he wasn't satisfied. He screwed up his face and glared at George. "You gonna listen to some saddlebum or your own brother and sister?" He pointed to me.

So, that's who Miranda was, their sister. But I still had no idea what George meant when he cautioned me not to mention Kate to her.

I shrugged and handed George a genuine bill. "Don't take my word, George. See for yourself."

Every muscle in George Weems's massive body grew tense as he read the words on the authentic bill. Slowly, he crumpled the bill in his hand as he made a fist the size of a sixteen-pound sledgehammer.

When he spoke, his words were low, but deliberate, but his voice quivered with restraint. "Albert, you're my brother. Because you are, I ain't going to kill you this time. But you just wasted twenty thousand dollars, so you're going to stay in this room and print up twenty thousand more with the right words on them. If you leave before you make them, I reckon I will kill you dead."

Albert stared at his older brother. "You can't mean all that, George. After all, it was just a little mistake. What would ma think if she could hear how you're talking to me?"

George's biceps bulged, stretching his cotton shirt. With ice in his voice, he replied. "Ma would probably help me beat your punkin head off, Albert."

George Weems might be an outlaw, but one thing I admired about him was his restraint. The way his body was shaking, he would have busted up anyone or anything he hit. He was mad enough to jump a twelve-foot fence and stomp a hole in the ground. But, he held a tight rein on his temper.

He pointed to the press. "Now, get busy, and don't come out until you finish." George glanced at Lorenzo. "You help him."

Lorenzo nodded hastily.

Back in the front room, George downed a full glass of whiskey, shivered mightily, and poured another.

Slowly, he shook his head and stared out the window. In a level, thoughtful voice, he said. "I swear, one of these days, I probably will have to kill that boy. I don't know what's wrong with him." He turned back to me as I poured two fingers into my own glass. "He don't use his head. He don't think. He just ups and does whatever he fancies at the time. Why, if I'd done something like that, my pa woulda stomped my carcass into the ground."

I took a sip of whiskey and tried to smooth the troubled waters. "It's not that much of a delay. Besides, suppose you'd had all five hundred thousand printed up and then found the mistake? Or what's worse, suppose we hadn't found it. What do you think those old boys back East would have done?"

George frowned. He hadn't thought of that. "They'd probably be mighty put out."

I chuckled. "Put out isn't quite the right words, George. Killing mad is probably a lot closer."

He tossed down the second glass of whiskey. "Reckon you're right about that, Curly. I'm much obliged."

"Anytime." I glanced around. "You don't mind, I'd like to wash off this trail dust and scrape off my beard."

"Sure thing. Follow me. I'll introduce you to the boys."

"The boys?" I pulled up. "You mean, there's more in this deal that just the four of us?"

George laughed. "They don't know nothing about what goes on up here. This here is a regular ranch, and they're my hands. That's why I figure it best you bunk out there. They'd be curious of a stranger sleeping at the main house. Since you'll be back and forth to San Antone, I've told them you're buying and selling cattle for me."

The bunkhouse was in much better repair than the main house. The only hand around was the cook, a wizened old Mexican named Diego Sierra whose face had more wrinkles than the Sierra Madres. "He ain't much to look at," laughed the broad-shouldered ranch owner. "But he's the best greasybelly in this part of the state. Keeps the coffee hot, and his grub sticks to your ribs like mud on a hog."

George didn't lie about Diego. The old Mexican was a dandy cook, right down to the bean pie. I'd turned up my nose when he offered it, but after that first taste, I put three hefty slabs away. Kind of reminded me of sweet potato or pumpkin pie.

Afterward, I bathed in the creek, taking care to keep my head out of the water. I shaved and changed into a set of clean duds and hung out my old ones to dry.

The rest of the afternoon, George showed me around the ranch, introducing me to the other hands as we ran across them. We reined up on the edge of a bluff overlooking a sprawling valley. "You got a fair operation here, George. Man could do right well with a spread like this."

"I reckon, but I never could see no sense in working myself to a nub when money's out there just for the taking." He pulled out a bag of Durham and built a cigarette, then tossed me the bag. "We're in the same boat, Curly. The law's after both of us. They just ain't got enough on me yet." He paused and glanced around as if expecting someone to be eavesdropping. "And I don't figure to hang around until they do. I plan on making a killing with this deal and then headin' for South Amurica."

"Sounds good." I'd never acquired the taste for tobacco, but apparently Curly Caruthers had. I hope I looked like I knew what I was doing. I curled the thin paper with my finger and sprinkled tobacco in it.

"What do you plan to do with your share?" Before I could reply, he added. "You know, Miranda's kinda got her cap set for you. That evening in Fort Worth put stars in her eyes."

I spilled half the bag of Durham on my saddle at those words. "Oh?" It was the reply of an idiot, but at that moment, my hands were shaking so badly I could barely roll the cigarette. How far had this business with Miranda progressed? "She's sure a looker," I muttered, wondering if that was the reply the real Curly Caruthers would have given.

George frowned as he turned his pony back to the ranch. He spoke over his shoulder. "Well, I don't know so much about that, but I reckon we all see things like we want to see them."

"I reckon." I managed to hold the match steady enough to light the cigarette, but it was so poorly rolled, that by the third or fourth drag, it fell apart. At least, George was riding in front of me and had not witnessed the demise of my cigarette.

Pulling my pony up beside George, I attempted to ferret out some information. "My manners aren't top-notch, George, but that night in Fort Worth, I had a little too much of the tiger. I'd be mighty displeased if I did anything to upset Miranda."

He laughed. "I don't reckon you could of done nothing to upset her. Next day when we headed back here, she said that evening was the best she'd ever spent. She just wished it could of been longer. She was sorely disappointed when you had to leave."

I grunted and fell silent. A single evening. That was all. But, that created another problem. What excuse was I going to use to go into Bandera for my ten o'clock meeting with my contact? George would understand a night out to howl, but what about Miranda? Or, would Curly really care what Miranda thought?

Of course, I couldn't afford to offend anyone, her or her brother.

On the other hand, I hadn't seen a woman around the ranch earlier. Maybe Miranda was away for the night.

She wasn't.

Miranda and Lorenzo was waiting on the porch when we rode up, and immediately I recognized her as the woman on the buckboard in town that morning. That's why she had been staring at me so hard.

She had changed out of the men's clothing into a blue calico dress that could have been fetching on a slender woman, but Miranda, I saw, was not what a feller could call slender. In fact, she and Lorenzo could have been twins. Even her red hair stuck out straight from her head. Her biceps matched his, ripple for ripple. Her chest—well, not to be indelicate, but it too matched Lorenzo's.

She smiled demurely and offered me her hand. "Howdy, Mr. Caruthers. It's good to see you again."

"H . . . Howdy."

She took my hand and led me into the front room.

I was as jumpy as a ten-legged spider. George offered me a shot of whiskey, but I declined. I couldn't afford to fuzzy my thinking.

"Won't you have a seat, Mr. Caruthers?" She gestured to one of the four ladder-back chairs in the room.

"Thanks." I nodded, glad to get a step or two away from her.

George cleared his throat, and with a grin, said, "I got something to look at out in the barn. I'll be back d'reckly."

I came close to panicking then, but I held my composure. "Don't you need some help, George?"

His grin broadened, and he glanced at his sister

who was smiling at me. "Nope. I got all *I* can handle."

No sooner had he closed the door, than Miranda
squealed, dashed across the room and leaped into my
lap and gave me a big, wet kiss. "Oh, Curly," she
said breathlessly. "I'm so glad to see you." Ignoring
the grease, she ran her fingers through my hair and
locked her arms around my neck. "I missed you so
much."

Well, sir, I didn't know what to do. Here was a
woman climbing all over me who I didn't know from
Adam. I just couldn't get into the spirit of the moment.

Suddenly, one of the chair legs snapped and sent
us sprawling on the floor. She landed on top of me,
and her stiff hair poked me in the eye. I rolled over
and managed to unlock her arms from around my
neck. Gasping for breath, I climbed to my feet and
helped Miranda to hers.

Immediately, she tried to throw her arms about my
neck again, but I held them. "Wait a minute," I whispered desperately. "What about your brothers?"

She paused, then gave me a knowing grin.
"Okay." Without a word, she poured two glasses of
whiskey straight and handed one to me. "Here. Drink
this while we figure out how we can get rid of them
like we did in Fort Worth."

My eyes popped open wide then. In Fort Worth?
"What . . . ah . . . What are you talking about?"

"You know, silly. The excuse you gave George
about going to Kate's. Albert overheard you talking.
George never has figured out that we met later that
night." She giggled and pressed her shoulder against
my chest. "Don't you remember?"

"Oh. Yeah, who could forget . . . that?"

My brain was racing. According to Rozell, Curly

had gone to Kate's. That's where he was arrested. It didn't take any genius to see what that low-down coyote was up to. He spent his time with Miranda, lied to her, and then hightailed it over to Kate's.

"It was the most wonderful time of my life," she whispered, leaning harder against me.

"Yeah. I know." I had to come up with a good excuse to get out of there, and fast. Otherwise. . . . I shook my head. I didn't even want to consider otherwise.

I downed half of my whiskey, shivered when it hit my belly like a firestorm, and said. "I'd like for us to get together, but I've got to go into San Antone tonight."

"Tonight?" She looked up at me, her eyes wide with disbelief. A frown twisted her face.

As I studied her face, I saw a hardness beneath the surface, and from time to time, a steely gleam glinted from her eyes. Miranda Weems was a tough woman. "Yeah. George wants me to make contacts back East. I've got to send some telegrams to line up buyers for the goods."

She considered my answer several seconds. Slowly, the frown faded into a smile. She stood on tiptoes and touched her lips to mine. "Tomorrow."

Gratefully, I nodded and backed away. "Tomorrow."

Outside the door, I ran into George. He smiled. "Heard what you said. You need any help?"

"Nope. I'll ride in. Hang around a day or so for answers."

"In the meantime, we'll be printing greenbacks . . . with the right spelling." He hesitated. A frown darkened his square face. "There's something you need to watch out for, Curly."

Now what? As if I didn't have enough to keep me occupied. "What?"

"The Knott boys. They hole up out west of Bandera. They been trying to push us out, but we don't push. Should they jump you, put some lead in them. That's what they'll try to do to you."

I tried to appear unconcerned, figuring that's how Curly would react. "Thanks. I'll watch for 'em."

When I rode out a few minutes later, heading southeast, I was wound up tighter than a rattlesnake. I think if even a grasshopper had fluttered past, I'd of drawn down on it.

A couple miles from the ranch, I stretched a rope neck high across the road, not in anticipation of the Knott brothers, but of Albert or Lorenzo. I still had the feeling that George didn't trust me.

I dug my spurs into my pony. The sound of his pounding hooves filled the evening.

After a quarter mile, I pulled into the underbrush to wait. In the distance, I heard the muffled thunder of hooves. Suddenly, a faint scream echoed down the road, followed by silence. I grinned, hoping the scream had been Albert Weems's.

Swinging east, I circled the Weems's Ranch and headed for Bandera. Within a couple hours, Special Agent Phillip Rozell would have his information, and I'd be five thousand dollars richer.

Chapter Six

There was no moon. The stars illumined the countryside with a cool, dim glow, painting the small town in stark relief. The only lights in Bandera came from the two saloons. I sat on the hill overlooking the village and listened to the off-key piano music stumbling through the night like a drunk.

In the next few minutes, my job would be over, just as soon as I passed on the information Rozell wanted. Still, I remained cautious. No sense losing a winning hand by being careless. I studied the layout of the town for my safest route to the blacksmith.

Down in the valleys and along the streams, large oaks spread their arched limbs. On the rocky bluffs and rolling hills, shin-oak and cedar struggled to sink their thirsty roots into the rocky soil, resulting in stunted growth. That's what lay between me and Bandera, a hillside choked with cedar and oak, offering excellent cover.

I dismounted and led my pony down the hill, not straying beyond the head-high cedar and scrub oak. Lights from the rear of the Empty Bucket threw yellowed rectangles on the hardpan behind the saloon.

A couple minutes later, I pulled up and stared into the shadows behind the blacksmith shop. Silently, I tied my pony to a small cedar and squatted near the edge of the growth, knowing that my shadow would be lost among the bulk of shadows formed by the oak and cedar.

Time passed slowly. I glanced at the Big Dipper. Past ten. I began to have second thoughts. What if my contact didn't show up? What if I had to keep playing this game?

The thought of a night ride to San Antone through all this underbrush didn't really appeal to me, but if something had happened to my contact, that's exactly what I would have to do to keep George from becoming suspicious. No two ways about it, George Weems would have one of his brothers in San Antone to keep an eye on me.

A movement in the shadows behind the shop caught my attention. A soft whistle startled me, then I realized it came from the rear of the blacksmith shop.

Leaving my pony back in the cedar, I dropped into a crouch and hurried across the hardpan and buried myself in the shadows. ''Where are you?'' I whispered.

''Here,'' said a woman's voice.

My muscles tensed.

Before I could speak, she continued. ''I've been waiting for you. You're late.'' She stepped forward, and the starlight lit her blond hair. ''I've got to get back to the saloon before they miss me.'' She giggled, and her voice dropped into a lower tenor. "I told them I had to go to the comfort room."

I tried to speak, but all I could do was babble. A saloon girl. She was my contact?

She spoke up sharply when I didn't reply. "What're you babbling about? Didn't you hear me?"

"Yeah," I managed to gasp out. "Yeah, I heard you. I heard you. But . . . I . . . "

She chuckled. I couldn't see her face for the shadows, but I imagined she was smirking at me. "You didn't expect a saloon girl to be your partner. Is that it?"

"Ah . . . well, yeah. I reckon that's it. I didn't expect a sa . . . " I hesitated, uncomfortable using that tag for her now. "I mean, that you was my contact."

She laughed again, soft and understanding. "Listen, cowboy, I been with the Secret Service three years now. This is just a role I'm playing, and if you want to win this game, you treat me just like you would any saloon girl. You understand? That's the only way we can get this job done."

I managed to relax somewhat. "I suppose. But, it don't make no matter anyway. I've got the information Rozell wanted."

For a moment, she was silent, then she said. "What information?"

"About the counterfeiting." I glanced over my shoulder. The tinny music continued battering the night. "Weems has a printing press set up in the back room of his house." Quickly, I told her what I had discovered. Each word brought me closer to the end of my job. By the time I finished my story, I was grinning like an egg-sucking hound who just found himself all alone in the henhouse.

Her blond hair bobbed as she nodded. "You did a good job."

"Thanks. And now, I'm going to wash this grease out of my hair even if I do go bald. But first, how do I find Rozell and go about collecting my money?"

She chuckled again. "It's not that easy, Jim . . . Curly. Maybe I'd better call you that instead of Jim. I'm Lucy. For the time being."

I didn't like the feeling that suddenly came over me. "Okay, Lucy. But, what about my money? How do I collect?"

"Sorry. But you don't. Not yet, anyway."

A flash of anger singed my words. "What do you mean, not yet? I did what Rozell said. I got him information and told him where to find the evidence to stop George Weems."

Her voice grew soft. "I know you did, Curly. But, a couple days before you got here, I received word from him to tell you that he wants you to make the contacts back East. Set them up, and then you're free." She paused. "He said he'd add another five thousand to the first five."

"That just ain't right," I said, every muscle in my body quivering and shaking like I had the chills. "We had a deal." I glared into the shadows that hid her face.

Lucy stepped into the starlight. Her brows were knit, her forehead, wrinkled. "I know you did, Jim. I'm sorry I had to be the one to pass along the bad news. I wish I could have told you where to pick up your money. But, Phillip Rozell is one of those men who'll stop at nothing to catch a lawbreaker."

"Even lying to a man?" My words snapped out bitter with resentment.

She laid her small hand on my arm. "Even lying to a man." Her words were soft with compassion.

"What if I say no?"

She blew through her lips. "He said if you balked, I should mention Judge Redstone."

I shook off her arm. "I reckon I'll have to get used to you people lying to me. How does he expect me to make those contacts back East? I don't know anything about counterfeiting or those who do."

"Don't worry," she snapped back. She handed me an envelope. "Inside are your instructions. They will tell you exactly what to do once you reach San Antonio."

"San Antone? Why there?"

"Because, Mr. Caruthers, that's the nearest telegraph."

For a moment, we glared at each other. Then, without a word, she brushed past me and disappeared through the rear door of the saloon.

I reached San Antone just before sunrise, stabled my pony in the first livery, and climbed into the hayloft for a short nap. When I awoke at noon, I was soaked with sweat and covered with a fine layer of hay dust.

My stomach growled like a hungry mongrel, so I pulled the hay out of my greasy hair, climbed down from the loft, washed off in the horse trough, taking care not to wet my hair, and ambled across the plaza to a small cafe where I knew the only choice on the menu would be chilies and beans.

The best I can say about the beans and chilies was they were filling. I leaned back and ordered a second cup of coffee and pulled out the envelope containing my instructions. I was still furious with Rozell and Lucy. They played me for a sucker. What made me even angrier was I couldn't do a thing about it.

I opened the envelope and pulled out the sheet of instructions. As I read the detailed set of directions, which also included a crude code Rozell expected me to use, I shook my head. It was obvious he had all of this planned from the beginning. ''That no-good, lop-eared . . . '' The sight of Lorenzo Weems riding down the middle of main street interrupted my ranting and raving about Phillip Rozell.

Quickly, I stuck the envelope in my shirt pocket and peered from around the edge of the window as Lorenzo pulled into the livery and asked the hostler some questions. He glanced over his shoulder in the direction of the cafe and reined his pony around, heading on up the plaza.

In one corner of the square, he rode through the open doors of another livery. Moments later, he reappeared and crossed the plaza, disappearing from sight.

So, I had been right. George had me followed. I sipped the coffee, making my plans.

Upon leaving the cafe, I wandered down the street toward the telegraph office. Siesta time, the town square was empty. Even the boys under the cottonwoods playing *pitarrilla*, a type of checkers, had vanished. But as the day cooled, the plaza would once again come alive with laughing *señoritas* and dashing *caballeros*.

From the corner of my eye, I spotted Lorenzo pull back behind a *careta* heavily laden with sacks of grain, chilies, and corn shucks to be used as mattress stuffing.

I ignored him, instead, continuing to the telegraph office where I sent a simple message to Rozell in Dallas, *Made it. How's the family? Chapman.*

After paying the operator and giving him instructions where he could find me, I took a room on the second floor in a small hotel and settled down to wait. I'd never had any truck with telegraphs, so I couldn't guess how long I'd be stuck here waiting for answers.

About mid-afternoon, I spotted Lorenzo leaning up against one of the cottonwoods in the plaza. I couldn't resist grinning. Despite the shade cast by the tall trees, his freckled face was as red as one of those hot chilies I ate at dinner. He removed his hat and wiped the sweat from his brow. Inside the hotel, I was fairly comfortable. Adobe does an excellent job maintaining a steady temperature day or night.

I must have dozed, for a knocking at the door awakened me. Outside, the sun had set. Reaching for my six-gun, I said, "Who is it?"

A boy's voice replied. "A message, *señor*. From *Señor* Castille at the telegraph office."

Opening the door, I took the folded message and tossed the boy a coin. "*Gracias.*"

Quickly, I stepped back into the room and peered out the window in time to spot Lorenzo buttonhole the boy and ask him some questions. Once or twice, he glanced at my window with a frown on his face. Finally, he shrugged and released the boy. Moments later, he headed for the nearest cantina.

I opened the telegram. As I expected, it was a conglomeration of letters that made no sense until I fit them into the code Rozell had provided. A wry grin played over my face when I imagined the confusion in the mind of Mr. Castille, the telegrapher. Nothing but four lines of gibberish.

Deciphering the message was simple. Within five minutes, I had all the information I needed. I had to hand it to Rozell. He knew his business. He provided me the names and addresses of five contacts back East. I stared at the names. "Who are they, Rozell?" I muttered more to myself than aloud. "Hombres who've been smart enough to dodge you, and this is the way you're going to set them up?"

A tinge of guilt depressed me, but I pushed it aside. I didn't have a choice. It was either them or me.

The room was growing dark. I closed the shutters and lit the coal oil lamp. My eyes locked on the small yellow flame licking at the inside of the lamp globe. I thought of the old gambler who had raised me, Larimer H. Harrison. "What about it, Larry? I don't even know these jaspers, yet I'm setting them up for a spell in prison. It don't make me feel any too good about myself."

And for a brief moment, I could imagine his face before me with that old mischievous gleam in his eye. "You play the hand you're dealt, boy. You play it the best you can."

And that's exactly what I decided to do.

Lorenzo Weems choked on his beer when I walked into the cantina and waved at him. His cheeks colored until the freckles all blended together in one red patch.

"Howdy," I said cheerfully. "Didn't expect to see you here." I slung a leg over a chair and plopped down at his table. "Want another beer?" Before he could answer, I ordered each of us one.

"Uh . . . yeah. Sure. Uh . . . uh . . . yeah. Thanks." I could see he was having a little trouble stringing his words together.

"Well, I don't know about you," I said, patting my belly. "But my chilies and beans is down to my toes. You want some?" I motioned to the little *señorita* waiting tables.

Lorenzo finally strung a couple words together. "I guess."

He was jumpy, fidgety as a crib girl in church.

"Albert come with you?" I asked innocently.

"No. He . . . uh, well, he got hurt. Fell off his horse."

I suppressed a grin. "Not serious, I hope."

"No, no. It ain't serious." He glanced around the cafe, just as if he was looking for someone.

"What happened?" I couldn't resist asking.

He cleared his throat and glanced around the cantina. "Oh, nothing. He just fell. That's all. He just fell."

"He get the money printed up like George wanted?"

Lorenzo paused to study the question. "Yeah," he finally said. "Yeah. He got it printed up."

The little *señorita* brought our meal, and we dug in, poking down mouthfuls of beans and chilies and washing it all down with a couple of mugs of beer.

Once or twice, I tried to get another conversation started with Lorenzo, but I reckon our previous talk had drained his bucket of words. Other than a *yep*, or *no*, or *reckon*, he had nothing to say.

My plate clean and my belly full, I pushed back from the table. "That's enough for me tonight. I got to be down to the telegraph office early in the morning." I winked at him. "Got some business to take care of."

He grinned and winked both eyes at me. I nodded and pushed through the door into the night air. Someone, somewhere back in his family tree must have been missing a few marbles.

I walked around the plaza for a few minutes, sorting my thoughts. First thing next morning, I would send five telegrams with the same message, the one Phillip Rozell wrote for me. I had memorized it. *New merchandise. Twenty-five to one hundred. Half million. Respond. CC San Antonio.*

The gay lilt of a fandango halted me in front of a hotel. I made my way through the hotel lobby to the patio where several laughing young *señoritas* and *caballeros* danced furiously. I watched for several minutes, thinking how wonderful it would be to be carefree again.

Reluctantly, I turned back to my hotel. As I crossed the plaza, I spotted Lorenzo still seated in the cantina, but now with a young lady at his side. ''Yeah,'' I muttered. ''And I thought he was on the slow side.''

My room was dark as the inside of a cow. Too tired and weary to bother lighting the lamp, I opened the shutters for the cool starlight to spill in. Without bothering to pull back the covers or shuck my boots, I plopped down on the bed and stretched out.

In the next instant, something struck against my boot from beneath the covers. In the back of my mind, I knew exactly what it was.

Chapter Seven

Rattlesnake!

Once in Abilene, Kansas, I saw a magic trick where a pretty young woman was levitated, made to rise into the air, while hoops were passed over her to prove no lines were holding her in the air. Well, sir, I added a twist to the trick.

The best way I can describe what I did after that snake bumped my boot was to say I levitated straight up off that bunk about six feet, shot to the left about six feet, and came down in the middle of the floor with my six-gun in my hand.

My hands shook so bad, I had to lay my six-gun on the table to steady the other hand so I could light a match. Just as the lamplight filled the room, a five-foot rattlesnake slithered from under my covers and plopped to the floor.

His tongue flickered, and he turned toward me, wrapping himself into a tight coil. I didn't want to kill him. Whoever planted him was around, and I wanted them to think they had succeeded. Just why, I wasn't sure, but somewhere in that frantic mind of mine, I had the idea that maybe someone would give himself away.

I holstered my six-gun and turned the straight-back chair over, holding it by a leg and using the back to pin the rattler's head to the floor. He squirmed and twisted, but I managed to grab behind his spade-shaped head and in one fluid move, tossed him out the open window.

Suddenly, screams broke out below the window. "Yahhh! Snake! Snake! Snake!" Gunshots rang out, and the night was filled with stomping boots and running feet. Just as quickly as the commotion erupted, it died away. And then the last sound I heard was the splintering of wood as someone ran through a wooden fence without bothering to open the gate.

Carefully, I inspected the room, every corner, every nook, every cranny for more snakes. Then I pulled the shutters and locked them from the inside. I could do without fresh air for the rest of the night.

I didn't sleep much that night. Every little sound jerked me up in my bunk. Finally, I lit the lamp and went back to sleep.

Rising early, I threw open the shutters and stared at the ground below. There was no snake carcass, but there were bloodstains on the ground below my window. They led to the shattered fence.

"I reckon you old boys'll think twice before you play with rattlesnakes again," I muttered, heading downstairs, anxious for a cup of steaming hot coffee.

At the base of the stairs, the sound of hammering stopped me. At that moment, the hotel clerk happened by. He quickly explained that the hotel was building a new privy, that the wood in the old one was rotten.

I thanked him, and headed across the plaza to the cafe. While I sipped my coffee, I tried to figure who wanted to get rid of me. Not George. He needed me. The only hombres I could come up with were the Knott boys, and I didn't know anything about them other than what George had said.

About that time, Lorenzo sauntered in. I waved him over. He hesitated. "Come on over," I called out.

He sat at the table gingerly, glancing nervously over his shoulder.

"What's wrong, Lorenzo? Something got you spooked? Couldn't be that little *señorita* I saw you with last night, could it?"

His face paled, and his freckles stood out just like he had the measles. "What . . . What *señorita*?" Then too fast, he added. "I ain't got no *señorita*."

Now I realized why he'd been so jumpy. "Well, now, I could swear I saw you in the cantina last night with a pretty young filly with long black hair. And the only females I've seen around here are *señoritas*."

His eyes grew wide with fear. "Please, Curly. Mr. Caruthers. D . . . Don't tell George. He'd whup up on me good if he knowed I'd been seeing Estrella. I . . . I promised him I wouldn't see her when he sent me to. . . . "

"To what? Keep an eye on me?"

His pale cheeks colored, and he ducked his head. "Yeah. To keep an eye on you." He looked up quickly. "But I wasn't keeping an eye on you. I . . . " He glanced around the cafe nervously, groping for the right words. "It's just that George would . . . well, you know."

I stared at him for several seconds, embarrassed that I had alarmed him so much. "Don't worry, Lorenzo. I won't say a word."

He grinned and sighed with relief. "Thanks. I . . . I owe you."

"Well, maybe you can tell me about the Knott brothers. You seen them around town since you got here?"

Lorenzo reached for his six-gun. "They here?"

"I don't know. I wouldn't recognize them. I got a feeling they might be."

He relaxed somewhat. "Why do you say that?"

"Someone stuck a rattlesnake in my bunk last night."

"Sounds like the kind of low-down trick they'd pull."

"So, you haven't seen them, huh?"

"Nope, but you can bet your last dollar, I'll keep an eye peeled for them."

"How many are there?"

"Three. The oldest is Leadbelly. He got that moniker cause that's where he shot a couple old boys a few years ago, in the belly. He likes to brag about it. His brothers are Cockeye and Bighead. Bighead, he's dumb as a skunk, and Cockeye can look two ways at the same time. All three is bad mean."

I drained the remainder of my coffee and pushed back from the table. "Come on down to the telegraph office with me. I want to hear more about these Knott boys.

By the time I sent the telegraphs, and we had sauntered across the plaza and squatted in the shade of the cottonwoods to watch the boys start up their first round of *pitarrilla* for the day, Lorenzo had filled me in on the Knott gang.

Having settled in Bandera County five years earlier, they promptly set out to prove they were the roughest, toughest, meanest collection of outlaws in Texas. Unlike the Weems boys who committed no crimes in their own county, the Knott gang rustled and robbed wherever and whenever they felt like it.

Suddenly, Lorenzo grew silent. He dropped his head and stared at the ground. "There's two of them right now," he whispered. "Under the *portales* across the plaza."

I glanced casually across the square and studied the flow of men and women walking in the shade of the arcade. Immediately, I spotted two men, one of whom leaned on a crutch. "That them? The big hombre with the crutch and the smaller feller?"

Lorenzo glanced up, then quickly looked away. "That's them. Cockeye and Bighead."

"Well, well, well," I muttered, watching their progress along the arcade until they reached the cantina.

Like most westerners, I'm easygoing. I don't look for trouble. In fact, I much prefer the peace and solitude of a shady tree on the bank of a creek brimming with fish. But, on the other hand, I never liked for a jasper to think he had me intimidated.

This spy business was getting confused. Sometimes, I wasn't sure if I was me or Curly. The role I was playing was coming mighty close to being the same role Curly would have played. I knew when we got back to the ranch that Lorenzo would tell George about the incident, and if Curly Caruthers did not respond in the manner he should, George would wonder why. Perhaps even grow suspicious.

Yet, what I was going to do was for Jim Wells, not Curly Caruthers. I wasn't thinking about George Weems's suspicions, but of my own good feelings about myself. The old gambler who raised me demanded I never bully a man, but he also insisted I never let anyone bully me.

I rose to my feet, brushed the dust from my clothes, and sauntered across the plaza to the cantina. I forgot all about the man I was impersonating. I was Jim Wells, greasy hair and all, and mad as a hive of stirred-up hornets.

The cantina was dark and cool. Other than Cockeye and Bighead bellied up to the bar, the room was empty. Now that I was closer to them, I realized the smaller jasper wasn't small after all. He was about my size, normal size. He just looked small because his brother, Bighead, was so large.

Lorenzo pushed in behind me, accidentally brushing against my shoulder. "Sorry," he muttered.

At the sound of his voice, the two men turned to face us. A slow grin spread over Cockeye's face. "Hello, Lorenzo. Fancy seeing you here." He was trying to ignore me, but one of his eyes kept flicking in my direction. The other one seemed to bounce all over the room.

Lorenzo nodded. "This here's Curly Caruthers, Cockeye."

Cockeye arched an eyebrow. "So. That supposed to be important to me?" He elbowed Bighead who laughed and shifted his weight from one foot to the other. Immediately, he winced, and shifted the weight back to the first foot.

I suppressed a grin. There was a bullet hole in his boot. So, one of those wild shots last night nicked him. When I spoke, my voice was so cold and icy, it surprised even me. "I'd say I was important, especially for you to take time to dump a rattlesnake in my bunk." I stepped closer and stared him in the eyes—I mean, in the eye. One eye looked at me, but the other seemed to have a mind of its own. It just kinda gazed around the room like it was trying to make up its own mind where to settle.

His grin turned into a smirk. "Sorry, cowboy. But,

we don't know what you're talking about.'' He looked up at his brother. ''Do we, Bighead?''

Bighead laughed, a solemn, deep-throated yuk, yuk, yuk.

''Sorry to hear that,'' I replied. ''It was a good joke, and I had a surprise for you, but if you weren't the ones I was looking for.... ''

The grin on Bighead's face disappeared. He looked down at Cockeye. ''You hear him, Cockeye. He's done got a surprise for us for the joke we done him.'' He turned back to me, and with childlike glee, said, ''What kinda surprise, mister? Huh? What kinda surprise you bring us?''

Cockeye turned mean. ''Shut up, you big dummy. He's joshing you. He ain't got no surprise for us.''

I held my arms out to my side, palms up. ''Oh, yes, I do.''

Before either one could reply, I stomped as hard as I could on Bighead's wounded foot, and threw a left cross into Cockeye's jaw.

Bighead screamed in mortal agony, grabbed his foot with both hands, and went hopping around the cantina while Cockeye and I went at it.

My blow spun Cockeye into the bar, but he bounced away and threw a wild right, which I ducked and shot a short right into his belly. He backed away a step and stared at me. I think he was staring at me. I couldn't figure out which eye to follow.

''Why, you.... '' He clenched his teeth and stepped forward, swinging an overhand right that I walked straight into.

I stumbled back over a table and sprawled on the floor. Cockeye rushed forward, raising his boot to stomp me, but I kicked a chair into his legs, and he fell forward.

Rolling to my feet, I threw a worried look at Bighead, but he was still hopping, still holding, still shouting.

Cockeye rushed forward. Two more times he popped me. I'd think a blow was coming from one direction. I'd duck, and that eye of his rolled around, and here came a fist from a completely different bearing.

Next time I didn't duck. Instead, I threw my own fist, and it caught him on the point of the chin. He backpedaled, but I stayed right on top of him, throwing lefts and rights as fast as I could into his belly and chest.

Suddenly, I stepped back and swung from the floor. I caught him on the chin, and he dropped like a sack of oats.

Chest heaving, I turned back to Bighead who was still hopping and shouting. He was too big to fool with, so the next time he hopped past me, I busted a chair over his head.

He shook off the blow, turned slowly to face me with a puzzled frown. He raised his hand and pointed a sausage-sized finger at me. "You . . . shouldn'ta done that." And his eyes rolled back in his head, and he collapsed.

Out back of the livery, I washed off.

"They ain't going to like what you done to them," offered Lorenzo, looking on like a dutiful son as he handed me a rag to dry my face.

"Maybe that'll remind them to leave us alone."

He shook his head. "Nope. Won't do it." He patted the wooden handle of his six-gun. "I reckon we'll have to kill them," he said matter-of-factly, just like a man would say 'let's go fishing.'

Other than the war, I never killed a man. In the war, a bunch of soldiers were never certain if they did or not. Minié balls flying everywhere. That was a different kind of killing. But, outside the war, I had never killed a soul, and I didn't plan on starting now.

"Don't you reckon?" he asked when I didn't immediately reply.

I dried the back of my neck with the damp rag. "Well, it looks like that, I guess, but there's a couple things we need to think on first." I was stalling for time until I conjured up a good reason not to shoot the Knott boys. "You boys have kept your noses clean around this part of the state, right?"

Lorenzo's brow knit as he struggled to think. It appeared a mighty battle was taking place inside that head of his. "So?"

"Just this." I squared my hat on my head, glanced around suspiciously so he would think I had a big secret to tell him, then lowered my voice. "What happens if someone sees us kill them? They might then forget about all the good you boys has done them. They might decide to chase you right back to the ranch. What would George think if *you* led a posse right into the house where he was printing up all that money?"

He tried to absorb all the words I had thrown at him. I could see he was quickly drowning in them, so I tossed him a few more. "Besides, you cause trouble in San Antone, you can't come back and see Estrella."

Well, that last flood of words pulled him under. "Yeah. I see what you mean," he replied. "But, if we don't kill them, what'll we do when they try to get back at us? And they will," he added.

Now, that was a question that truly had me buffaloed. My first reaction was to run like the devil, but I couldn't leave until I got word from those five jaspers back East. How long it would take them to reply to my telegram was anyone's guess, but I had to hang around until then.

"Let's just wait and see." I patted my six-gun. "You oughta go on back to the ranch."

"I can't. George told me to stay with you."

"Well, then, just stay away from back alleys. I figure that's where Cockeye and Bighead usually handle their business."

Chapter Eight

All five prospective partners responded before the sun set. Each jumped at the plan, but each made a counteroffer on the price. I wired them that there would be no discussion on price. The offer was good until noon the next day, then it would be taken from the table.

A banging on my door awakened me the next morning. "What do you want?" I yelled.

"It is me, *señor*. From the telegraph office. *Señor* Castille, he has sent me with messages for you."

The room was dark. I glanced toward the window. Through the shutters, I saw false dawn lighting the sky. Gun in hand, I padded across the room and opened the door.

"Here, *señor*." He stuck a handful of paper at me. I tipped him and closed the door.

Lighting the lamp, I read the telegrams and grinned. Each one accepted the deal and gave an address to where the merchandise should be delivered. I grinned and slapped the palm of my hand with the telegrams. What else could Lucy and Rozell want from me now?

I folded the telegrams into my pocket and reached for my boots. Nothing was keeping me here now. A large bowl of chilies and beans, a pot of black coffee, and I'd head back to Bandera.

Clomping downstairs, I turned out back toward the privy. I was no more than half a dozen steps out the back door of the hotel when a storm of gunfire rang out. Slugs grabbed at my shirt sleeves, tore up the ground at my feet.

In one motion, I leaped behind the new privy and shucked my own six-gun. Another hail of lead ripped apart the corner of the wooden building. When the gunfire momentarily subsided, I stuck my arm and head around the corner and squeezed off a couple shots while I tried to pin down the location of the bushwhackers. I found them quickly. They were firing from inside the old privy.

A slug whistled past my ear. I fired twice more and rolled back behind the new privy.

Rising to a crouch, I reloaded my Army Colt and considered my options. All I had to do was wait, and help would soon arrive in the form of the sheriff or some other citizens. Maybe. Or, if I could drive them out, set the place on fire or something, then I could hightail it while they were distracted.

"Bighead and Cockeye," I muttered, guessing at the identity of my bushwhackers. Lorenzo told me they'd try to get back at me. Maybe he wasn't as dumb as he put on.

I removed my hat and peered around the opposite corner of the privy. For a good two seconds, I studied the ramshackle building in which the Knott brothers hid. Then another storm of gunfire ripped into the new lumber in front of me. I dropped to the ground and waited.

Then I grinned. I couldn't set the privy on fire, but I knew how to drive them out. In the couple seconds I had studied the old structure, I spotted a wasp nest the size of my hat in the open eaves of the privy. Large, red wasps. The kind that would chase me for a mile when I was a kid.

My grin grew wider, and I waited for them to re-load. A few seconds later, the firing ceased. I imag-ined them breaking open their six-guns, ejecting the spent cartridges. About at the time I figured they would be fumbling in their belts for fresh cartridges, I stepped around the corner and emptied my Colt at the nest.

The first two slugs tore chunks from it, and the third one tore it down.

I jumped behind the new privy and quickly re-loaded while I waited for the fun to begin.

The early morning was silent, calm.

Then screams ripped the silence apart, followed by the sound of stomping boots and slapping hands. ''Get'em off me. Yahhh! Watch out.''

And then a different sound joined in with their screams. Wood cracking. Beams breaking, snapping.

''Out,'' one of them shouted. ''Get out of here.''

But it was too late. The popping of stressed lumber giving way drowned his words. All I heard then was one or two blood-chilling howls.

I glanced around the corner of the privy just in time to see the old outhouse collapse into the pit below, carrying with it two screaming bushwhackers.

By this time, several curious onlookers had gath-ered, and as one we all approached the pit with some trepidation. The smell was overpowering. Two or three of the brave souls turned back, but I was just curious enough to see if my suspicions were true.

They were.

Clinging desperately to pieces of the outhouse with one hand and swatting at wasps with the other, the two Knott brothers were neck-deep in the muck, screaming for help. The frantic hotel clerk found a rope and tossed it to them.

I didn't bother to hang around. I had to get back to Bandera and turn over my plans to Lucy and Rozell. I had accomplished what they had asked.

Lorenzo was waiting for me on the Bandera road, and together we reached the ranch just before sunset. My own feelings were mixed. When I rode away from the ranch a few days before, I had not planned on returning. That was before Rozell changed horses on me mid-stream.

Now, here I was, feeling a whole lot like Daniel entering the lion's den or the standard-bearer for the Light Brigade.

George or Albert didn't worry me, I could handle them. But, Miranda . . . She was the joker in the deck. How well did she know Curly Caruthers? That was what bothered me.

And she was possessive. I saw that right away. The way I figured it, she and Curly had some kind of agreement, and she was bound and determined to hold him to it, which meant she would probably keep those beady black eyes of hers locked on me.

If all that was true, I'd have the Devil's own time getting to Bandera alone.

And all my guessing turned out to be right on the money.

She was awaiting my arrival in that same blue cal-ico dress. Her red hair still stuck out straight, and when she grinned that first time, I saw that she had lost a front tooth.

"Damned wide-eyed bronc," she muttered. "Trying to top him off, and he popped me right into a tree limb."

I clucked my tongue and shook my head in feigned sympathy. But to be honest, the missing tooth sort of improved her appearance, like one of those pirates with the patch over his eye.

She grabbed my arm and pulled me toward the house. "Come on in. There's time for a drink before supper."

George just grinned, but I managed to extricate my arm from her web of hands. "I'd like to, but I got to look after my horse." I backpedaled while I babbled.

"I can do that for you, Mr. Caruthers," chimed in Lorenzo.

"No. No," I replied hastily. "He picked up a stone, and he's sensitive about his feet. I'm the only one he'll let fool around him like that."

"I'll give you a hand," Miranda said, hurrying forward.

"No. No. You stay in the barn . . . I mean the house. Fix me that drink. I'll be right back in."

She paused, glanced at George who was still grinning like a boar hog in a mud hole. "All right," she said, trying to sound demure.

I sighed with relief. Being alone with her in the house was bad enough, but the barn?

While I tended my pony, I considered my situation. It had been uncertain enough earlier, but now with the added problem of Miranda's infatuation, I had the feeling I was in the middle of a big stew that was ready to be stirred up. To top it all off, there was nothing I could do about the whole mess except keep blundering forward.

* * *

Around the supper table, Lorenzo filled George and Albert in on all that had taken place in San Antone.

When he finished, I laid out the deal I had made with the five distributors back East.

George gave Albert a smug grin. Then to me, he said. "And each wants a hundred thousand?"

"That's right. They'll pay off when we deliver."

Albert tried to speak, but only a strangled garble came out. He shook his head angrily at George.

"What happened to him?" I asked innocently. I had earlier spotted the rope burns across the neck.

"Run into a tree limb is what he told us," Miranda said. "Of course, he couldn't talk, so he just writ it out."

I shrugged in sympathy. "Too bad, Albert. Man's gotta be careful of those tree limbs. They can be downright dangerous if a man isn't careful."

Miranda nodded emphatically. "Oh, Mr. Caruthers. You're just as right as rain, ain't he, George?"

"Reckon if you say so, Miranda," he replied, suppressing the grin on his face.

Everyone of us there except Miranda knew exactly how Albert had run into that 'limb,' but none of us would mention it.

Albert scrabbled for a piece of paper and wrote furiously for a couple minutes.

George read the message and pushed it across the table to me. *look out fer trap. them boys back east is full of tricks*

After reading his note, I looked at Albert. "You're right. We got to watch ourselves."

My agreeing with Albert put him off balance. The anger on his face was replaced with confusion. I'd given him a second thought to hold in his head, and he couldn't handle it. Old Albert, he had a one-thought brain.

I turned to George. "You tell me when we'll be ready, and I'll set up a date with our customers." I paused, then added. "Don't worry. I'll set it up so our backs are protected. Federal prison doesn't hold any attraction for me."

"Sounds okay with me." He screwed up his square face in concentration. "I reckon we oughta be done in a couple weeks. If nothing don't go wrong."

"Well, then, I'll ride back and wire them not to expect to hear from us for two weeks. Then we'll be set."

Miranda spoke up. "Not tonight? I thought . . . " She hesitated and glanced around the table. "I mean, I just figured you'd be too tired after riding all day." It was a lame excuse, but it saved her face.

George chimed in. "Yeah, Curly. Miranda's right. Why don't you hit the sack early, then light out before sunup. You'll be good and rested like that."

I was hemmed in. If I insisted on going, George would become suspicious. I'd just have to figure another way to get into Bandera. "Good enough for me." I rose and nodded. "If I'm going to leave that early, I'd better climb into my bunk."

Miranda's eyes widened, but she remained silent. I could almost visualize the thoughts running through her head.

At that moment, I was faced with one of the most difficult decisions I've ever had to make. Glancing at the puzzled look on George's face, I quickly lined up all the if's, and's, and but's, then held out my arm. "Of course, if you don't mind, George, Miss Miranda might enjoy an evening stroll . . . just a few minutes," I hastily added. "Wouldn't want to keep her out late."

How she did it, I don't know, but before I could say another word, she had bounded across the table and wrapped her arms around mine.

That was the first time I had ever taken an evening stroll with a young woman on a dead run. She tried to pull us into every shadow we passed. Most of them I dodged, but once or twice she won out and managed to plant a big, wet kiss on me.

A couple times, we stopped and chatted. At least, I chatted. Miranda kept locking her arms around my neck and running her thick fingers through my greasy hair. I felt her running her fingers over my skin behind my right ear, but I paid no attention.

That was a mistake I would regret.

Once, she drew back and stared up at me. The starlight hit her full in the face, and I could see the frown on her forehead. "Are you all right, Curly?"

"Sure," I replied, laughing. "What makes you think I'm not?"

She shrugged. "I don't know. You don't seem the same like you were in Fort Worth."

Chills ran up my back. That's all I needed, to blow this whole deal just because I wouldn't pay her the attention she wanted. I hugged her to me. "No, I'm the same. It's just that we've got our entire future riding on this plan. I don't want to see it shot to pieces."

With a giggle, she hugged me. "I'm sorry. I guess I'm just being silly."

I finally got her back to the main house after making a heap of promises I had no intention of keeping. On the way back to the bunkhouse, I couldn't help feeling sorry for Miranda and disgusted with myself for leading her on.

Yet, I had no choice. Phillip Rozell had me pinned to the wall. But I made myself a solemn promise that as soon as he turned me loose and I had the ten thousand, I would bust him between the eyes.

I rode out early next morning, well before sunrise. An hour out, I pulled off the trail and wound up the rocky slope to an oak-sheltered ledge overlooking the trail. Putting coffee on to boil, I waited, curious as to whether George had sent Albert or Lorenzo after me this time.

No one followed.

After an hour, I rode on, excitement pumping adrenaline through my veins. The sooner I reached San Antone, the sooner I could set the time and dates for the meetings, and the sooner I could settle up with Lucy and Rozell.

I rode into San Antone just before sunset. Within an hour, I had the messages sent and was putting myself around a large steak. After supper, I ambled down to the cantina and had a couple of drinks and set in a poker game for a few minutes.

Later, I strolled the plaza, enjoying the soft warm breezes, the smell of harvested fruits, and the music of fiddles and guitars.

Under one of the cottonwoods, a laughing *caballero* spoke to a coy *señorita*, and for a moment, I was envious of the couple. No vagabond was he. He had a home, someplace to hang his hat, stable his horse.

And that was exactly what I would have, I promised myself that night. Just as soon as I finished my job for the Secret Service.

I'd find me a nice spread of grassland along the Colorado or the Guadalupe. Ten thousand dollars would put me in good shape. Maybe a thousand acres. Still leave me five thousand dollars or so. I could pop wild longhorns out of the brush and cross them with some of those newer breeds.

Yep, soon, maybe I could have a good life.

Chapter Nine

By noon the next day, I had all my times set. Using the information given me by Phillip Rozell, I set payoffs in Atlanta, Washington, Philadelphia, Jersey City, and Boston for the second week in August. That meant we had to have all the merchandise printed by the last week of July to give us the travel time we needed.

Then I headed back to Bandera. Along the way, I committed the list of payoff spots to memory and tore up the paper on which the information was written. Now, I had an ace in the hole.

For once in my checkered life of dumb stunts, I had made a smart move.

Four hours out of San Antone, three highwaymen stopped me, their faces covered with masks, which failed to hide their identity. Not even a gunnysack could conceal the bulk of Bighead Knott, which meant the other two gunnies had to be his brothers, Cockeye and Leadbelly.

When I spotted the muzzle of one revolver pointing off to my left instead of directly at me, I knew I was facing Cockeye.

The third masked man did the speaking. His voice gargled, like he was trying to carry water in his throat while he talked. "Don't try for the six-gun, mister. Your carcass won't be able to hold all the lead you'll catch."

That seemed a sound enough argument for me to keep my hands well away from my Colt. Were they planning to get even for the beating I gave Cockeye? Or for their less than memorable bath in the privy?

I forced a weak grin. "Don't worry . . . Mister Knott." My reply startled him. His forehead wrinkled. Before he could respond, I nodded to the other boys. "Afternoon, Bighead, Cockeye. See you boys got yourself all cleaned up."

Cockeye yanked his mask off and shouted at his big brother. "I told you masks wouldn't fool this hombre, Leadbelly. There ain't no sense in foolin' around with him. If he don't give us the information, shoot him dead."

Now, those words really caught my attention. I hastily smoothed at the troubled waters. "Well, boys, I don't know what you're after, but I'm perfectly willing to share whatever I got. Without no argument. There's coffee in the saddlebags along with a new Ned Buntline dime novel called *Buffalo Bill's Last Victory*." I nodded to their six-guns. "Just be careful with those hoglegs."

Leadbelly yanked his own mask down, revealing bleary eyes, sunken cheeks, a bulbous nose spider-webbed with blue veins—a face ravaged by alcohol and hard living. "Just don't you get too smart, mister. I got a head on my shoulders too."

Nodding quickly, I replied. "Yes, sir. I see that you

do. And it's a mighty fine-looking head, if you don't mind me saying so. Besides, I'm not smart at all, not at all. It's just that I couldn't help recognizing your brother there.'' I looked at Bighead. ''I reckon there's nobody else in this part of the state the size of Bighead.''

Well, Leadbelly digested those words for a few moments, then grunted. ''Okay. Give me your six-gun. Handle first.''

I did exactly as he said, holding the muzzle with my thumb and forefinger, keeping my pinkie extended like I was at some fancy dinner.

He grunted. ''Now, let's go. Ride up ahead of us.'' He waved the muzzle of his six-gun at me.

''Whatever you say.'' I headed up the trail toward the Weems ranch. The Knott brothers rode behind. I had no idea where we were going, but at least I had the time to formulate a plan, if you can call leaping from my saddle a plan. That was all I knew to do. Jump into the underbrush before they started taking potshots. At least it was a chance.

After fifteen or twenty minutes, Leadbelly shouted. ''That's far enough.''

My muscles tensed, and I strained to hear the click of hammers being cocked.

Leadbelly shouted again. ''Take the trail to your left.''

I groaned with relief and reined my pony up the ascending trail.

Ten minutes later, we rode into a small clearing in front of a cave from which a small stream of water gurgled.

''That's far enough. Get down.''

The clearing had been used before. Looking around, I could see why. Good graze for the horses.

A panoramic view for miles. Snug quarters against the weather.

I dismounted and turned to face the three brothers, not knowing whether I could expect a beating or a shooting. Naturally, I preferred neither, but one thing was certain, they didn't go to all this trouble just to offer me a spot beside the campfire.

One thing I knew for sure, they weren't going to gun me down first. They wanted something, or Leadbelly wouldn't have sent them into San Antone the first time.

Bighead had not spoken during the entire ride. No sooner had we dismounted, however, than he limped toward me, a smug grin on his face. He smacked a large fist into the palm of his hand. "Can I hurt him now, Leadbelly, huh? Can I?"

Cockeye leered at me.

Leadbelly replied, a gleam in his own eye. "Not yet, Bighead. When I tell you. When I tell you." He fished in his saddlebags and pulled out a half-empty bottle of whiskey. "No, we'll first see just how much Mister Caruthers here is willing to tell us before we get rough." He turned up the bottle and chugged four or five swallows.

"Boys," I said with a grin wide as the moon. "Like I said before, I'm perfectly willing to share anything I have with you. There's no need to resort to violence."

Bighead frowned. I doubt if his vocabulary consisted of many more words other than *kill*. But Leadbelly understood. He grinned. "Well, I'm glad to see you want to make it easy on yourself."

"Yes, sir. I firmly believe in making it as easy on myself as I can. Whatever you want ain't no skin off my nose."

He nodded to his brothers, then pointed the whiskey

bottle at me. "What did George Weems hire you for?"

I'd figured that might be what had him so curious, and I'd come up with several explanations, but by now, Phillip Rozell had me lying to everyone, and sooner or later, those lies were going to trip me up. But, I had to have a plan, one that stuck close to the truth. "Counterfeiting."

Cockeye looked up at his older brother. "Do that mean what I think it means?"

Leadbelly's eyes narrowed. "You lying to me?"

"Nope. Like I told you. It's no skin off my nose." I hoped my plan worked.

The thought of counterfeiting intrigued Leadbelly. His eyes glazed over and for several seconds, he was lost in thought. The rest of us just stood there and stared at him like we had good sense.

He cleared his throat. "Counterfeiting money?"

"Yep. That's . . . That's what he's counterfeiting. Money."

He looked at Bighead and Cockeye. "Get a fire going. Caruthers here's got coffee in his bags. Him and me's going to talk."

We squatted in the mouth of the cave. He handed me the whiskey bottle. "Now, tell me about this counterfeiting."

That bottle was passed back and forth several times before I finished the story. I told him all about the press, about the plans for selling the merchandise, even about the contacts. Of course, I didn't tell him everything about our prospective customers.

And, I set everything back a month. That and the list of contacts I had committed to memory were my two aces in the hole, one to take care of the Knott boys and the other, the Weems boys.

"Why should I believe you?" Leadbelly asked when I finished.

"Go ask George."

His eyes bugged out, and his jaw dropped open. "What do you think I am, some kind of fool? He'll draw down on me soon as he sees us."

I shook my head. "Not if you go under a white flag and with a note from me."

He eyed me suspiciously. "A note from you? What about?"

"Asking him to come here so we can all talk this out. Between you and me, there's plenty to go around. After all, twenty-five percent of four million dollars is two million split two ways. Figure it up." I crossed my fingers, hoping he was as dumb as I thought.

Leadbelly screwed up his bottle-worn face as he tried to cipher out the figures. After a few moments, he nodded. "That's a heap of money."

I grinned to myself. My plan was going to work. "Like I said. Too much for just one family. Plenty to go around."

He studied me a few more seconds, still suspicious. "How do I know you're not lying to me?"

"Leave me here with Bighead. You and Cockeye take the note in and bring George back here, but . . ." I hesitated and stared him straight in the eyes. "You got to agree there won't be any shooting."

The glitter of a new idea leaped into Leadbelly's eyes. I quickly plucked the gleam from his eye. "You don't know how to do the counterfeiting. George does. That's why you can't kill him."

Leadbelly sagged back against the cave wall. "Okay. Write the note."

I tore the cover from the Buntline dime novel and wrote the note using a .44 cartridge.

George
I am safe. Come with Leadbelly. Deal is off if you do not follow these instructions.

Curly

After Leadbelly and Cockeye rode out, Bighead glared at me. "My brother told me not to hurt you. But, he said if you tried to run away, I could break your leg." He flexed his thick fingers and grinned.

"Don't worry, Bighead. I won't cause you any trouble." I pointed to my saddlebags. "I'm just going to get my book about Buffalo Bill and sit back and read it."

His eyes lit up. "Buffalo Bill? I heard about him and all them circus acts. Is that book really about him?"

"Yep. All about him."

He coughed once or twice, then cleared his throat. He glanced at the ground. "Would . . . I mean, could you read it to me? I . . . I can't read none."

I grinned. "Sure. Pour us some coffee while I get the book."

Within thirty minutes, I had a lifelong friend, an overgrown, carefree puppy who had the bad luck of being in the body of a giant . . . of a giant, I reminded myself, who would break my leg if I tried anything.

After we finished the novel, Bighead busied himself shaving some jerky into a pot for broth while I moved my horse to another graze. He had been feeding toward a thick tumble of poison ivy and poison oak.

I wasn't worried about him. He'd never eat ivy or oak, but more than once, he brushed up against some and gave me a case of it.

A hour later, George rode up with Leadbelly and Cockeye. He reined up and looked down at me. "You hurt?"

I was squatting against the trunk of an oak, sipping coffee. "Nope. I'm doing just fine." I held up the cup. "I hope you got something stronger to flavor Bighead's coffee. It's a tad weak."

He fumbled in his saddle bags and tossed me a full bottle. "Now, what's this all about?"

I topped off my cup and corked the bottle. "Climb down, and I'll tell you about it." As he dismounted, I said to Leadbelly, "Give me a couple minutes to explain to George what I did."

Cockeye spoke up. "You talk in front of us. We don't want no secrets here."

Giving Leadbelly an innocent grin, I explained. "Now you know, Leadbelly, that I told you every-thing without talking it over with George here. Nat-urally, George will be upset. Wouldn't you be?"

Leadbelly frowned. "I reckon."

"So, all I want to do is explain it to George so he can see that the plan you and me made is best for everyone. Now, don't you think that's smart?"

He glanced at Cockeye who was staring at the bot-tle in my hand and the setting sun, a trick only Cock-eye could master. "What do you think?"

Cockeye refocused his eyes. Now he was staring at me and at my horse off to the right. "I don't trust him."

"Well, they ain't goin' no place, and I don't figure letting them talk will hurt nothing." Leadbelly nod-ded to the edge of the clearing. "Say what you got to say."

I grinned and took George's arm. "Over here, George. I've got something to explain."

For a moment, he resisted.

I dropped my voice to a hard whisper and dug my fingers into his arm. "Come on, George. It's impor-tant." I almost yanked him off his feet.

He stumbled after me. "This had better be good."

We stopped at the edge of the clearing. "Now, listen," I began, keeping my voice low. "These Knott boys are looking for trouble, and trouble's the last thing we need now. Everything's set for our plan, the dates, places, payoff, everything. We just keep going like we've planned." I paused and grinned at Leadbelly and Cockeye who were watching us with growing suspicion. "Smile at them," I whispered.

George grimaced. "What?"

"Grin at 'em."

"Hell, no. I hate their guts."

"Enough to lose a hundred and twenty-five thousand dollars?"

"I'll grin."

The two Knott brothers visibly relaxed when George smiled at them.

"Keep grinning," I said, continuing my explanation of how I had deliberately set everything back a month. "We'll all be out of here by the end of July, long before Leadbelly knows we're gone. It'll be September before he figures out what's taken place. All we have to do in the meantime is play the game."

George eyed me warily. "What about the ranch? He won't see none of us there."

"But, he'll see your hired hands. Didn't you say you were getting out of the state? Let your men run the ranch for you. Never can tell, you might want to come back in the years to come."

He grunted. "That's smart." He poked me in the chest with his finger. "But don't get too smart, Curly. A .44 don't measure smart or dumb."

"Don't worry, George. Just play along with the plan. It'll all work out. Now, go shake hands with Leadbelly. Tell him you agree to the plan."

He hesitated.

"Remember. A hundred and twenty-five thousand dollars."

He shook hands with Leadbelly.

The next thirty minutes, we sat around the campfire with the Knott boys swapping lies and drinking whiskey.

Finally, George climbed to his feet and stretched. The sun had slid behind the trees. "Well, Leadbelly. Reckon it's time Curly and me leave. It'll be well after dark before we reach the ranch."

"Yeah," I said, chiming in. "And why don't you boys ride over tomorrow and see the layout. That oughta make you feel better."

Leadbelly grunted. "All that'll make me feel better is my share of two million dollars."

"By the way, Leadbelly. You still got my Colt." I held out my hand.

For a moment, he eyed me, then with a grin, slipped the six-gun from his belt and tossed it to me. "See you tomorrow."

"Okay." I noticed they had made no preparations to leave. "You boys staying here tonight?"

"So what? You got a law against it?" Cockeye snapped.

I swung into the saddle. "So nothing. Just figured if you were, there's a nice bed of soft leaves over there that would make a nice mattress tonight."

As we rode away, I glanced back in time to see Bighead gathering an armload of poison ivy and oak and carry it to the cave.

Chapter Ten

We reached the ranch before sunrise and went immediately to the main house where I wrote out a list of addresses and dates for the payoffs.

George held it to the lamplight and read it. He grinned at me. "If I was of a mind, I could take advantage of you now, Curly." He tapped the list with a finger. "I've got all the information I need here."

I poured us each a drink. "Yep. But, I trust you, George."

George laughed, a full-bellied, rollicking laugh. "One thing you never have to worry about, Curly, is me. I told you before, I'm an honest outlaw. I ain't going to trick you."

I touched my whiskey glass to his and downed the drink. Darned if I wasn't coming to like the giant of a man.

Back in the bunkhouse, I slept in fitful snatches until mid-morning for I couldn't decide just how to get the details of the plan to Rozell. What excuse could I give for riding into Bandera?

Lorenzo provided me my answer.

He was sitting at the trestle table in the bunkhouse with a scowl on his face when I climbed out of bed. I stretched and reached for the coffeepot. "What's eatin' you?" I asked.

His scowl deepened. "Today's the Fourth of July. I wanted to go to town for the fireworks, but George told me I couldn't."

"Huh. Why not?"

Lorenzo dug at the table with a fingernail. "Oh, I don't know. He don't want to go, and he thinks I'll get in some kind of trouble."

A weight slid off my shoulders. There it was, the perfect excuse. "Too bad. Sounds like fun," I replied, sitting across the table and sipping the thick, Arbuckle coffee.

His face brightened. "It does? Would you like to go? I mean, if you was to go, George wouldn't mind me tagging along."

I yawned and tried to play uninterested. "I don't know. We could get out in the yard and shoot off our six-guns. Be about the same thing."

"Oh, no. They say they's going to have rockets this year. You know, them big things that shoot up in the air real high. I saw one a couple years ago. It was a sight. Will you, Curly? Huh? Will you?"

I sipped my coffee before answering. "Well. If George don't mind, I'll ride in with you."

"Wow-ee," he exclaimed, leaping from the table and racing toward the main house.

Smothering a grin, I watched him. Perfect. Get him to watching the fireworks, and I'd slip off, give Lucy the information, and skip out of town.

"Oh, no," I gasped.

Lorenzo frowned. "What?"

I stammered to cover up the words that had burst out on their own upon hearing Lorenzo's announcement. "I mean, oh, no, too bad George isn't going with us."

"Oh, yeah, but that's okay. Miranda's going instead. We'll have a good time."

"You bet." I nodded and groaned silently. "You bet." Now, I had two problems, Lorenzo and Miranda. Lorenzo, I could ditch, but Miranda—nobody ditched Miranda.

Miranda, wearing her blue calico dress, climbed gracefully into the buckboard in one great leap. The seat under us groaned when she plopped down. She waved at George on the porch. "Sure you ain't coming to see the fireworks?"

George waved back. "Naw. I'll sit here and kill a bottle. Maybe shoot a couple rabbits."

One thing about George, he was always able to entertain himself. "So long," I yelled, popping the reins.

Lorenzo rode beside us on a nice mare. Miranda talked, and talked. I answered in monosyllables, trying to figure out just how I could get rid of her for ten minutes.

When we hit Bandera at sundown, Lucy was standing on the boardwalk outside the Empty Bucket. Lorenzo yelled and waved his hat at her. She gave him a grin and disappeared inside the saloon. Four or five cowpokes stumbled from the saloon, whiskey in one hand and a six-gun in the other.

And then I knew how to get away from her.

"Hey, Lorenzo."

"Yeah?"

"You ever been on a snipe hunt?"

"Snipe? What's that?"

I held my thumb and forefinger about two inches apart. "Little birds, about this size."

He shook his head. "Naw. I ain't never been snipe hunting. Why?"

"Just wondering," I replied. "Just wondering."

We rode on through town and pulled up beside several other wagons overlooking a large meadow. A cluster of cowpokes stood a short piece from us, sharing a bottle. "I'll be right back," I said to Miranda. "I want to talk to those old boys over there."

She frowned. "What about? You know them?"

"Nope. But, I figured this being the Fourth and all, maybe we can have fun."

Her eyes narrowed. "You talkin' about Lorenzo?"

"Yep." I grinned. "He's a good kid. He'll enjoy it."

She studied me. "Won't hurt him, will it?"

"No. We just show him how to call snipes in. He sits there with a bag until they show up."

"That's all?"

"That's it." I laid my hand on hers. "It's just fun. Don't worry."

The cowboys took to the idea like a fox to a henhouse.

Two or three of them wanted to start the hunt immediately, but others talked them into waiting until after the fireworks display.

The display lasted about thirty minutes, and as wagons headed back home, I took a drink out of the local bottle and passed it on to Lorenzo. "You say you never hunted snipes, huh? You want to?" Several grinning cowpokes had gathered around us.

"I don't know."

Several encouraged him. "Go ahead. It's fun."

He took a long drink and passed the bottle. "How do you hunt snipe?"

A young cowboy stepped forward. "Easy, Lorenzo. Here's a gunnysack. We'll find a good spot out there in the woods for you. You wait out there with the bag open and scratch a stick on the ground in front of it. The rest of us, we'll start driving the snipes to you."

"You bet. They shore make good eatin' too," drawled another cowpoke. I stayed in the background, letting the others carry the joke.

With his friends encouraging him, Lorenzo gave in. We started into the forest with him. As soon as I was out of Miranda's sight, I doubled around the small town and hid in the shadows near the blacksmith.

Minutes later, the silhouette of a woman stepped from the rear of the Empty Bucket. I whistled softly.

"Curly?"

"Yeah," I said, stepping from the shadows.

"Well, I see you're still alive," said a second voice, one I immediately recognized as Rozell's.

"Yeah. I'm still alive, and I got your information. I'll give it to you and you give me my money, and we'll call it quits."

He held out his hand. "What do you have?"

I gave him the dates and addresses. Holding them to the light, he read them. "Good." He folded the papers into his vest pocket. "As for you, there's been a change in plans. You're to go to Atlanta with them. Keep 'em from getting suspicious. We'll arrest you in front of them. That way, we don't blow our cover."

My ears roared. "Just a blasted minute here. That's not part of our bargain." I shot a dagger look at Lucy. "You told me this was it. I get this information, and I'm finished."

"I know," she said. "That's what I was told. I. . . ."

"She doesn't know anything, Wells. She's like you, a hired hand." He punched himself in the chest with his finger. ''We make the decisions, and our decision is that you either accompany Weems and the money to Atlanta, or you stand trial for bank robbery.''

I glared at the smaller man. I'd never wanted to stomp someone like I did him, but he had me where he wanted me, standing on slick ice with one foot. I tried to remain calm. ''How do I know you'll keep your word this time?''

He laughed. ''Here. Read this.'' He handed me a folded sheet of paper. ''That is signed assurance that Atlanta will be the last I ask of you, and that you did not have a part in the bank robbery in Dallas.''

I held the note up to the light from the saloon. It was what he said. Still, I was growing mighty tired of being lied to. ''Like I said, how do I know you'll keep your word on this?''

He sneered. ''You don't. But, what choice you got?''

''You better hope, Mr. Rozell,'' I said, studying him coldly. ''That I never catch you on level ground. I got no choice now. But, one day. . . . ''

Lucy stepped forward. ''Curly . . . I'm sorry. I. . . . ''

''Forget it,'' I barked. ''I've been kicked in the teeth before. I'll get over it.'' I gave Rozell one last, murderous look, and then disappeared back into the shadows.

Back at the wagon, Miranda asked. ''Where's Lorenzo?''

I nodded to the forest. ''Waiting for snipes.''

She grew thoughtful. ''I saw the others come back. They was all laughing.''

''Yeah.''

''And Lorenzo's still out there?''

''Yeah.''

''There ain't no such thing as a snipe, is there?''

I chuckled. ''No. There ain't, but it's a joke men like to play on those fellers they like. It's not a mean joke.''

She smiled, and in the moonlight, it was becoming. ''I'm glad. Lorenzo is a good boy.''

Chapter Eleven

During the ride back to the ranch, I tried to push my anger with Rozell aside. I had to slip back into my role as Curly Caruthers, for that was the first time Miranda and I had been really alone, and I was mighty uncomfortable. I had no idea what she might expect from me . . . from Curly.

But, all she did was keep her head on my shoulder all the way to the ranch. We talked, dreamed, made plans. Once or twice, I found myself envying Curly, not so much because of Miranda, but because he had the dream of every man within his grasp—a wife, a ranch, children.

When I helped her down from the buckboard, she gave me a light kiss and said. "This was more wonderfuller than that night back in Fort Worth, Curly. Thank you."

Later, lying on my bunk, I thought about Miranda, about her hopes and dreams, and I felt lower than a snake's belly. Finally, I dropped off into a restless sleep only to be rudely awakened by a bucket of cold water in my face.

Sputtering, I jumped to my feet. "What the. . . . "

Lorenzo was laughing. "That'll teach you to send me off on a wild-goose chase."

I laughed too, and the other cowpokes, now awake, joined in.

Luckily, I had been sleeping with my hat on, which kept the water off my hair. Otherwise, I might have jumped out of that bed a bald man.

Every time I thought I might nod back off to sleep, Lorenzo would start in with another version of his snipe hunt. All told, we had to listen to that story four times before the sun rose.

The next two weeks raced by faster than one of George's Kentucky thoroughbreds. In a way, I almost hated to see it end. I had grown attached to Lorenzo and Miranda, and even gruff George. Albert, well, only a mother could be attached to him, and then only if it was at the end of a ten-foot pole.

A couple of times, I found myself wondering if I could stop them, tell them the truth, maybe even straighten them out, but deep down, I figured that would do no good. Rumor had it they were killers, though George had denied it that first day. But they had robbed and stole, and no trail-drifting cowpoke like me was going to turn them around.

At the end of the second week, the Knott boys rode up, their pale faces covered with scabs. George and me were on the porch, enjoying the shade and the evening breeze.

George wrinkled his nose and chuckled. "You boys look like you got the mange."

Leadbelly shot Bighead a murderous glare. "This

idiot here put poison ivy under our blankets. You shoulda seen us last week. We's having to use match-sticks to prop our eyes open so we could see.''

I shook my head and glanced at Cockeye who was glaring at me and at the barn.

''The reason we come over,'' said Leadbelly, ''was to see how our deal is progressin'.''

''It's right on schedule,'' I said, stepping forward. ''We ought to have the entire amount ready to move by about the first of September.''

Bighead looked at Leadbelly. ''When's September, Leadbelly? Huh?''

Leadbelly waved him off. ''Later. Now, shut up.'' He turned back to me. ''How about taking a look at it. I ain't never seen that much money.''

He started to dismount, but I stopped him. ''Can't. It's already packaged. You see, as soon as we print up a hundred thousand, we package it and set it aside. That way, we stay organized with no problems. And you can't imagine the number of problems we have when we have to repackage the packages because the paper we use in packaging the packages gets stiff and is hard to break.'' It was a mouthful of nonsense, but I didn't want Leadbelly to see that we were in the process of shutting down the press.

Leadbelly paused with one leg hiked over the sad-dle. ''Oh. Well, that being the case, I sure don't want to cause us no problems.'' He straightened back into the saddle.

I grinned. ''Tell you what I'll do. Just before we ship it next month, I'll send you word and you can come over and take a look at it.'' I gestured to Cock-eye and Bighead. ''And bring your brothers. In the meantime, we best not be seen together. Don't want folks to get suspicious, do we?''

He sat up in his saddle and stared down at me, just

like he'd suddenly come up with an idea of his own. "Yeah. We better not see each other. We don't want folks to get suspicious." He hooked his thumb over his shoulder. "Let's go, boys."

As we watched the Knott boys ride away, George slapped me on the shoulder. "That was purty slick, Curly. I tell you, old son. At first, I was against you and Miranda hitching up, but now, darned if I don't figure you might make for a good old brother-in-law."

I grinned back at him. "Glad you think so, George. Mighty glad." A cold shiver ran up my back. This was the first time I'd heard anything about this marrying business.

I'd been lucky so far, but I crossed my fingers, hoping my luck held and Miranda was planning the wedding after the payoffs and not before.

The entire scheme was ticking off like a fine watch. The merchandise was all wrapped in wax paper and packed into individual suitcases that Lorenzo and me had brought back from San Antone the week before.

"Won't someone wonder why we're carrying so many suitcases on the train?" George asked when I explained the details of our trip.

"No. There's five of us. Each has one suitcase. We'll let Miranda have an extra one for her own ... well, you know, women things."

George considered my reply. "Oh. Yeah. I see what you mean."

As the time to pull out came closer, I grew more and more nervous. Three nights before we were to pack up and head for Dallas and the Atlanta train, I took a chance and slipped into Bandera to pass word along to Lucy.

When I started to leave, she laid her hand on my

arm. "I'm sorry you got pulled so deep in this mess, Jim."

I stared at her in surprise. "You . . . I mean, how did you know my name?"

"Rozell told me. He. . . . " She hesitated.

"He what?"

Lucy stepped closer. She had a fresh, clean smell about her, like the milky breath of a young calf. "Be careful. Rozell hasn't said anything, but I don't trust him. I hope, for your sake, he arrests you in Atlanta like he said."

Her words hit me in the pit of my stomach like the kick of a mule. I had considered the possibility that Rozell would double-cross me once again. "You think he'll leave me in there all the way to Boston?"

"He's low-down enough. I think he sees a big promotion for himself when he nails these jaspers. Rumor is that the man in Boston is head of the gang that runs everything from Boston down to Jersey City. If Rozell can nab him, he can just about name his own job in the agency."

I whistled softly. Why couldn't this be just a simple spy job? Now, it looked like we were getting into a game of hide-and-seek. "Thanks," I replied, laying my hand on hers. "You pulling out of here now?"

Lucy nodded. The moonlight bounced off her blond hair. "Yes."

"Well. Take care. It's been nice knowing you."

She chuckled. "You're not finished with me yet."

I frowned.

"When you get on the train, you'll see a black-haired woman wearing a black mourning dress with a veil over her face. She'll be with you all the way to Atlanta."

"You mean . . . ?" I pointed at her. "You . . . ?"

"Orders." She nodded. "Rozell wants someone

around just in case there's problems.'' Lucy glanced over her shoulder at the Empty Bucket Saloon. ''If you're leaving Friday, then I'm bailing out tomorrow. You best hope nothing goes wrong in the next couple days because you won't have a contact around.''

Palm down, I made a slow cutting motion with the edge of my hand. ''Everything's smooth as still water.''

And I thought it was until I put up my pony and stepped out of the barn into the early morning. A shadow rose from the ground in front of me.

''What the . . . ?'' I jumped back and grabbed for my Colt.

Miranda Weems spoke softly. ''Leave the six-gun alone. It's only me.''

''You scared the blazes out of me,'' I muttered, laying my hand over my heart. I chuckled.

But she remained serious. ''What have you done to Curly?''

My blood ran cold. ''What?''

''You heard me,'' she said, her voice edged with ice. ''You're not Curly Caruthers. What have you done to him?''

Chapter Twelve

I tried to laugh her accusations away. "What kind of trick are you up to, Miranda? Of course I'm Curly." I glanced nervously toward the main house.

She shook her head. "No. You're not Curly. I've known for a long time, but . . . I didn't want to say anything because you were so nice to me, not like Curly."

My head whirled with desperate lies. I could see my deal with Rozell falling apart.

"Is he dead?" Miranda's voice was soft and earnest.

Lying would get me nowhere. Somehow, she knew the truth. "No. He's still in prison. Me and him was put in the jail wagon in Fort Worth. He was still drunk, and he spilled the whole scheme. From Dallas, they moved him on to Huntsville. I spent three days in jail for disturbing the peace, and when I got out, I figured on taking advantage of the fact him and me looked so much alike." I hesitated. "And that's the story."

In the distance, an owl hooted.

Miranda remained silent.

"How did you guess?" I asked.

"It wasn't hard. Curly's mean, clean through. He'd knock me around. Not in front of George, but when we was alone."

"Maybe he changed?"

She shook her head and laid her thick fingers behind my earlobe. "Curly had a big scar right there. You don't have one. And, his hair was never as greasy as yours."

For several moments, we stood staring at each other. Finally, I managed to speak. "Now what?"

"I don't know." She ran her fingers through her mop of hair. "If I tell George, he'll kill you dead." She paused and studied the problem. "Maybe we should go through with the whole plan and then, if you wanted to, you could just fade away one night. That way, nobody'd get hurt."

I heard the emphasis she put on *if you wanted to.* Like every unhappy person, she was reaching out to someone for whom she cared, leaving herself open to hurt. I knew what she wanted me to say, but I couldn't—I couldn't lie to her like that. "Thanks." I laid my hand on her shoulder. "And who knows? Things could work out for everyone."

"Not for me. They never have." With a sad smile, she nodded and turned back to the main house. I felt like I was sitting on a keg of black powder, juggling a handful of burning matches. At any time in the future, for even the most insignificant of reasons, Miranda could spill the whole story.

That was Wednesday morning. The remainder of the day, I felt like I was tiptoeing through a barnyard filled with fresh cow patties, careful of every word, of every step. I didn't know what could set her off.

The next morning, Lorenzo and me rode into Bandera to pick up some of that newfangled barbed wire for the ranch. While I was waiting outside the general store, I spotted Lucy across the street.

She nodded behind the Empty Bucket, then disappeared down the alley.

I glanced inside the store. "I'm going over to the saloon and buy us a bottle, Lorenzo. Any special brand?"

Lorenzo waved. "Just as long as it's whiskey."

Quickly I crossed the street and without hesitation, headed out the rear. The bartender glanced at me, and I pointed to the back door. He grinned, figuring I was rushing to the privy.

Lucy was waiting just outside the door.

"What is it?" I asked. "I thought you were leaving."

Her face was pale and drawn. "I had to get word to you. Curly Caruthers broke out of Huntsville two days ago. He's heading this way."

I groaned. "Just when I thought things couldn't get any worse, they did."

"What do you mean?"

"Miranda Weems knows I'm not Curly."

"She what? How?"

"That's not important. Right now, she thinks I'm just a drifter who stumbled into a good deal. She's willing to ride it to the end."

Lucy laid her hand on my arm. Skepticism etched deep lines in her forehead. "Be careful, Jim."

"You bet," I muttered. "You bet."

Needless to say, I did quite a bit of damage to that new bottle of whiskey by the time we reached the ranch. I was ready to pull up stakes and dust Texas off my boots.

But I couldn't. I was in so deep that I figured I might as well ride the wide-eyed bronc until it threw me or I busted it.

Thursday evening, George and me sat on the porch, our chairs cocked back against the house. I pulled an accurate schedule of payoffs from my pocket and handed it to him. He opened it and frowned. "I've already got a copy of this."

"Not that one, George."

His frown deepened. "I don't understand what you're tellin' me."

I forced a grin. "I've got a confession to make before we leave, George. I want to clear the air. Early on, I figured you would try to double-cross me, so I changed the location of the last four drops." I nodded to the paper in his hand. "Well, I was wrong. You've been fair with me, and I'll be fair with you. That schedule is the real one."

He stared at me, then dropped his gaze to the paper in his hand. Without looking at me, he said. "With this, I don't need you anymore."

"That's why I gave it to you. So you would know that I trusted you completely."

His red head bobbing, he pondered the schedule, then slowly folded it into his pocket. A broad grin split his square face. "Obliged, Curly. I just want you to know that you don't have to worry about getting a square deal from me."

"Thanks, George. I was hoping you'd say that."

He reached in his pocket and pulled out a bag of Bull Durham. Silently, he rolled a cigarette and tossed me the bag.

Together, we sat on the porch and smoked our cigarettes as the sun set in the west. George was as contented as a young calf with a full belly. But, I was balancing myself gingerly on the edge of a razor, nervous, jittery.

Everything was set in place, ready to go. But, like a house of cards, the least gust of wind could blow it down on my head.

We pulled out the next morning. Around every bend, at the top of each hill along the road between Bandera and Dallas, I expected to run into Curly Caruthers.

Luck was with me.

We ran into several drifters, some of whom bedded around our fire, but they were all strangers. I had expected Miranda to act differently, but she didn't. Just like before. Kind of silly. Giggled a lot.

One thing I never could figure out though was why she never asked me my real name.

We reached Dallas six days later, on Thursday.

Friday morning, we climbed aboard a day-coach on the Atchison, Topeka & Santa Fe for the next leg of our trip. The only furnishings in the coach were hard, wooden benches, placed back-to-back in rows. We found a set of benches facing each other and quickly stacked our suitcases against the wall of the coach.

We had arrived early. Within minutes, the coach swarmed with cowhands hefting their saddles on their shoulders, rough miners heading for new fields, farmers buying supplies or selling harvests, teachers, ministers, and businessmen.

Miranda, wearing that same blue calico dress with the lacy cuffs and neck, looked around and wrinkled her nose. "Do we have to ride with all of this crowd?"

George winked at me. "Yep," he said "Just like Curly and me planned. The more jaspers we keep around us, the less likely we're going to draw attention to ourselves."

Just before the train pulled out of the station, a woman in black wearing a heavy veil boarded. She paused, looked the coach over, then slowly made her way up the aisle. I kept my eyes forward as she passed us.

Moments later, the coach shuddered, and with the clanging of its bell, the straining 4-6-0 freight locomotive with its balloon smokestack jerked its string of cars out of the station, bound east.

I grinned at George. "Next stop, Atlanta."

He nodded.

At a steady forty miles an hour, we chugged over the rolling hills and entered the piney woods of East Texas, leaving behind a tenuous ribbon of black smoke.

The clackety-clack of wheels over the narrow-gauge rails grew monotonous, lulling me to restless sleep, for Miranda's knowledge of my charade stayed at the forefront of my mind.

If I could just reach Atlanta before the scheme fell apart.

For two days, we sweltered in the coach during the day, and, at night, fought mosquitoes that were unnaturally attracted to my greasy hair and large enough to carry off a horse.

The train made frequent stops for water and fuel, giving weary patrons a chance to stretch their legs or partake of the numerous trackside eateries that dotted the right-of-way.

Lucy sat by herself at the opposite end of the coach, her mourning attire giving her privacy. A few caring ladies offered her sandwiches from their own meager supply or lukewarm coffee from the local trackside cafe.

The morning of the second day, I was staring out the window at the sunrise. Lucy had switched to a bench facing us. Her head was erect. Despite the veil, I knew she was looking at me, but I kept my eyes out the window.

Next to me, Miranda groaned. I glanced at her. What would she do when Rozell arrested me? Give me away? Or carry through with the deal? I guessed the latter. The Weems clan coveted money, and with me out of the way, there was just that much more for them.

We pulled into Atlanta just after noon.

I glanced around as we disembarked. Hoping Rozell would wait until I could distance myself from them, I picked up a suitcase and nodded to the cafe within the station. "I don't know about anyone else, but I'd like to put myself around a large steak."

George hesitated.

"We got time. Our meeting isn't until two o'clock."

After we ordered steaks and coffee, I excused myself. "I just want to check on the train schedule. Find out if the train to Washington is on time."

George nodded. Albert and Lorenzo were too busy staring at the bustling crowd to pay me any attention. Miranda just smiled.

To my surprise, I felt a pang of regret as I walked away from the cafe. I had grown attached to the family, and although I was protecting my own good name, I felt guilty about the trap into which I led them.

I sauntered up to the ticket agent, paused, and glanced around, expecting to see a horde of lawmen descending on me, but all I saw were busy men and women bustling in every direction.

For ten minutes, I loitered around the station, but no Rozell.

Suddenly, a hand touched my shoulder. I spun. "Where have you . . . ?" I clamped my lips shut.

Lorenzo was staring at me, puzzled. "Sorry, Curly. Didn't mean to spook you. I . . . I just wanted to tell you the food's here."

"Oh." I forced a grin. Where in the Sam Hill was Rozell? Had something gone wrong? "Thanks." I glanced around once more. No sign of the Secret Service agent. I clapped my hand on Lorenzo's shoulder. "Let's go put ourselves around those steaks. Okay?"

"You bet."

I didn't have an appetite. The last couple weeks, the possibility of Rozell failing to arrest me had squirmed around in the back of my head like a handful of worms. And now, it appeared my concern had become a reality.

The others ate with gusto, downing a pitcher of beer between them.

While they put themselves around the hearty meal, I tried to plan my next step. Our first meeting was with Duke Casement in the Alhambra Cafe one block north of the station. Casement and Caruthers had been friends, and there was no way on this green earth I could fool him. Fool him? Who was I kidding? I didn't even know what he looked like. So, how could I pick him out of a crowded saloon?

Across the table, Albert and Lorenzo were shoveling grub in their mouths with both hands. Miranda was no slouch in the food-gobbling business either.

I picked up my mug of beer and leaned back.

"This is a mighty busy train station, George. You noticed?"

He glanced around, then quickly returned to the half-eaten steak in his plate. "Hadn't paid no mind."

"Well, I have. It's busy, and with all the pick-pockets and thieves, and God only knows what else running around this place, I don't think it's a good idea to leave Miranda alone while we go to the pay-off.''

George grunted and kept eating.

"The Alhambra is one block north of here. Why don't you and the boys take a suitcase and handle the payoff. Miranda and I will hang around here and keep an eye on the rest of the merchandise.''

Looking from under his eyebrows, George replied. "Figured on taking her in there with us." He went back to his meal.

"In the Alhambra? That's a rough place, George. No place for a lady.''

He paused with his fork in mid-air. He appeared confused. He mouthed the words, *a lady*. Then he looked at Miranda who was glaring daggers at him. Slowly, his brain shifted into gear and ground out the obvious reply. "Good idea, Curly. You and Miranda wait here. We'll find this Casement bird without no problems. You just look after my little sister here.''

I grinned. "Good idea, George.''

While George and the boys were in the Alhambra, Miranda and I sat on a bench in the waiting room, five suitcases between us. "Taking no chances,'' I said, patting the leather portmanteau next to me.

"Who are you really, Curly?''

The question came out of nowhere, startling me. I hesitated, then replied. "Just a drifter, like I said.''

"No. I mean, your name. What's your real name?''

Taking a deep breath, I answered her. "Well, I guess you're entitled to the truth, Miranda. You could have told George about me, but you didn't. Bob Smith. That's my name. Bob Smith out of Abilene, Kansas.''

She arched an eyebrow. "That sounds like a made-up name to me.''

I laughed. "Shoot, Miranda. I've changed my name so many times that it's hard for me to remember, but that's it, honest and true, Bob Smith." I hurriedly cautioned her. "Just don't you go and call me that in front of your brothers, you hear?"

"Don't worry, I won't." She was silent for a moment. "Bob Smith. I like it. It has a good sound to it. What are your plans when this is all over?"

She was making me more than just a little nervous with this talk that was sounding more and more domestic. "Oh. I hadn't really thought about it. I . . . "

The ticket clerk's voice booming through the megaphone announcing the latest arrivals interrupted us.

"That reminds me." I stood up quickly. "Let me double-check to make sure our train is on time."

My brain raced as I wound my way through the crowd to the ticket window and took my place in line. The woman in front of me stiffened. She turned her head from side to side, sniffing the air. She looked back at me, and her eyes stared at my head. She wrinkled her nose and turned back around with a shudder.

I vowed right then to find the nearest body of water and jump in even if I came up bald.

Moments later, a low voice from behind startled me. "Rozell is dead." I started to turn, but Lucy whispered. "Don't move. Don't pay me any attention. As soon as you can, get out of here. Forget this deal."

The line moved forward. I whispered over my shoulder. "What about you?"

"I've been ordered to follow through on it."

"Follow through?"

"All the way."

"All the way? You mean . . . ?"

A voice interrupted me. "Yes, sir. Can I help you?"

"Huh?" my eyes focused. The ticket agent was looking at me.

"I said, can I help you?"

"Oh, yeah. Yeah. When is the next train to Washington?"

He consulted a handwritten log. "On time. Two forty-five."

"Thanks."

When I turned, Lucy had disappeared.

For several seconds, I considered my next move. Should I just walk out the door and keep going? I had Rozell's agreement in his own writing. But what about Lucy? The Weems boys hadn't killed Rozell. That meant another gang was involved. The Knott brothers? No. I didn't think so. But then, who?

I closed my eyes and felt the weight of the world settle on my shoulders. With a sigh, I headed back to Miranda and the train to Washington. If Lucy was sticking it out, I could do no less. I shook my head. What an idiot I was. The oil from my greasy hair must have soaked into my brain.

Chapter Thirteen

George and the boys returned with a wide grin on their faces. "Smooth as goose grease," said the older brother, patting the money belt around his waist.

"Glad to hear it." I glanced at the clock on the wall and casually said. "We'd better board. The train pulls out in fifteen minutes." I rose from the bench and helped Miranda to her feet.

Albert protested. "We got time. Besides, Duke Casement said he'd drop by the station to see you." The red-headed man narrowed his eyes, and a faint smirk curled one side of his lips. "He was disappointed you didn't show up. Reckon he wanted to talk about old times or something."

That's when I started tossing suitcases to them. "Let's get loaded aboard anyway. We want to find a seat."

"But . . ." Albert sputtered.

Miranda glanced at me, then shoved her suitcase in

Albert's stomach. "Stop gabbing and get us aboard. You want to miss the drop in Washington?"

The suitcase in his gut knocked Albert back a step. "Hey. Watch what you're doing there, Miranda. I'll slap you silly if you. . . ."

George grabbed the front of Albert's shirt and yanked him around. "You're the one who'd better watch out. You don't talk to your sister like that, you hear me?" George's face was red as a new pair of long johns.

Albert struggled futilely, but George's sausage-sized fingers held the younger brother tightly. "I mean it, Albert. She's our sister, and you'll treat her right, or I'll bust your cotton-picking head wide open. You understand me?"

The younger brother glared at George for several seconds, then dropped his gaze to the floor. "Yeah. I understand."

"Good." He looked around. "Now, let's get aboard that train."

He didn't have to tell me twice. I had a suitcase under either arm and one in each hand. "I'm ready," I sang out, heading for the coach.

The car was so crowded, we were unable to find five seats together. Miranda, George and I sat at one end of the coach; Albert and Lorenzo, at the other end of the coach.

The conductor, wearing his kepi hat and black uniform, strode past. I stopped him. "How long before we pull out?"

He fished his pocket watch from his vest and studied it. "Three minutes."

"Hey, look. There's Duke Casement," said George pointing at a small cluster of men stepping on the loading platform.

"Where?" I acted as if I didn't see them.

"There they are, just coming out of the station. There's Duke in front."

A short, heavyset man wearing a black and yellow checkered suit stood surveying the train. His handlebar mustache drooped below his heavy jowls. When he saw me looking through the window, he waved and started toward the coach.

I fought back the panic. I couldn't afford to chance meeting Duke Casement in front of George.

"Looks like he's coming aboard," drawled George.

"Yeah," I replied. "I'll go meet him. It's too crowded in here."

Without waiting for a reply, I headed for the door where I hesitated and glanced back. George and Miranda were watching Duke and not me, so I opened the door and slipped off the opposite side of the coach deck. Quickly, I hurried forward five or six coaches, and then climbed back aboard, deliberately remaining on the coach deck where I was within reach of the ladder that led to the top of the coach.

I sighed with relief. Duke Casement and his boys were somewhere behind me.

Then a jocular voice froze me where I stood. "Hey, Curly, you old son-of-a-gun. How you been?"

I looked around to see Duke and two of his boys grinning at me from the platform beside the deck. "Duke. Good to see you." It wasn't much of an imaginative greeting, but I was lucky to choke those words out of my mouth.

"Come on off there for a minute." He waved me to him. "I missed you at the Alhambra."

Reluctantly, I did as he asked, desperately searching for a way out.

He extended his hand. "Curly, you old dog. It's been a long time."

"Yeah, Duke. Longer than you know." I took his hand and shook so hard his mustache quivered.

The smile slid off his face. He cocked his head to one side and stared up at me. "Hey, you ain't Curly Caruth . . ."

I didn't give him a chance to finish his exclamation. With my right hand still clutching his, I jerked him toward me and whipped a left cross into his jaw. His head snapped around, and he sprawled on the platform.

His two cohorts jerked themselves from their stunned stupor and leaped at me. I ducked and they slammed into each other. I darted for the crowded station. Behind me, the groaning of the great steam engine, and the clanging of the bell signaled the departure of the train.

"Get him," a voice behind me yelled.

Outside the station, I dashed down the boardwalk, planning on ducking into an alley and leaping aboard the moving train. I zipped around the first corner and skidded to a halt, pulling up short just before I slammed into a vendor pushing a rickety cart loaded down with two black pots of steaming soup.

After squeezing past the cart, I raced for the train, which I could see at the end of the alley. Just before I broke into the clear, I heard a loud clatter, followed by screams of pain.

Hastily throwing a glance over my shoulder, I spotted the overturned cart and three men on the ground swimming in a pool of soup.

The train was picking up speed, black smoke churning into the air. I leaped aboard and looked square into the puzzled faces of Albert and Lorenzo Weems. I paused, caught my breath, and then grinned.

"Hiya, boys," I said, brushing past them without

any explanation. "Better get to your seats. Someone else might already have them."

George and Miranda were looking out the window when I sat down. They looked around in surprise. "Where'd you go?" asked George. "We kept looking, but we never saw you on the platform."

"Nowhere." I nodded to the front of the car. "We stood on the coach deck just outside the door and talked." Quickly, I changed the subject. "So, the exchange went off without a hitch, huh?"

With a broad grin, George patted his belly. "Twenty-five thousand."

I winked at Miranda. "Not bad for a morning's work."

She didn't reply. She just smiled and dropped her eyes, remaining subdued as she had been throughout the trip. In fact, ever since she learned I was not Curly.

Because we were at the threshold of our scheme that Wednesday night back at the ranch, I hadn't taken time then to wonder at her change in demeanor.

And presently, I had enough on my mind trying to figure out the Washington drop. This was one I was not supposed to have any part in.

Racking my brain, I pieced together the details of the next payoff. Like Atlanta, it would take place near the station, in a saloon called The Four Leaf Clover. The kingpin in Washington was an Irishman, Sean O'Toole. Since I was to have been arrested in Atlanta, Rozell had not bothered to brief me on the remaining drops.

The windows were wide open, and a hot breeze curled inside the coach, cooling the beads of perspiration on our foreheads and running down our backs. The coach rocked from side to side. I leaned back in the seat and closed my eyes, the clacking of the wheels pounding like a drum in my head. Soon the rocking and clacking became syncopated, eight clacks as the ponderous coach rocked to one side, then eight more as it rocked to the other.

Slowly, I pushed the rhythmic beat into the background and forced my numbed brain to function. With Rozell dead, my only contact, and the only person alive who knew the deal between me and the dead agent was Lucy.

Was she still on the train? She had to be. Those were her orders. Slowly, I opened my eyes and stared out the window at the passing countryside. Yawning, I stretched my arms and stood up. "Think I'll walk some kinks out of my legs." I looked at Miranda. "How about it?"

"No. Thanks." She smiled softly at me, and despite the bad break nature gave her with the Weems face, there was a glow about her.

"Reckon I'll take you up on that stroll," drawled George, rising and popping the knots from his joints. Noting the crowded aisles, he added. "How some ever, I don't reckon we'll walk too fast or too straight."

I grinned and rubbed the side of my legs. "Be hard to get used to this kind of riding."

"You're right about that, old son. You surely are."

Holding on to the back of the seats to steady us against the rocking motion of the coach, we made our way through the crowd and stepped out on the deck.

George rolled a cigarette and tossed me the bag.

We smoked in silence, George, I guessed, imagining the next drop and another twenty-five thousand dollars. Me, I wondered about Lucy. I hadn't spotted her in our coach. What if she had missed the train?

I looked at the right-of-way blurring past. With Rozell dead, all I had to do was step off, and I was out of the entire scheme. Find my way to the nearest settlement, buy a horse, and disappear into this vast country.

"Excuse me, sir," A feminine voice jarred me from my thoughts. I looked around and stared into Lucy's black veil.

Startled, both George and me stumbled back. I mumbled. "Yes, Ma'am. Excuse me."

She looked at George. "I . . . I apologize for disturbing you gentlemen. I needed a breath of fresh air, but I didn't mean to interrupt anything."

"Oh, no, Ma'am," George replied hastily, removing his hat. His red hair popped out like rusty springs. "It's right fine with me. You ain't botherin' us none at all, is she, Curly?"

"No, Ma'am," I replied.

She gave me a cursory nod, then turned back to George. "I'm not much of a traveler, I'm afraid. The coach is so sweltering."

George nodded. "Yes, Ma'am. An' it's mighty hot in there too."

Lucy slipped her fingers under the veil and tugged at her collar. "I don't mean to impose, Mister . . . I'm sorry, I don't know your name."

For a moment, a blank look crossed George's face as he tried to remember his own name. Then he caught hold of it. "Weems, Ma'am. Uh . . . George . . . yeah, that's it, George Weems." He nodded to me. "And that there is Mister Curly Caruthers."

"I wonder, Mister Weems, if I could impose on you to fetch me a drink of water."

"Yes, Ma'am. You shore can."

He shuffled around her and disappeared into the coach.

Lucy turned to me quickly. "What are you doing here? I told you to get out of this."

"Nope." I patted my vest pocket containing the note. "If you're going through with this, so am I. I got my letter that'll take care of me, but this could be dangerous. I ain't no hero, but I figure on keeping a hand in the game."

"You're crazy." She hesitated.

"What about these next four gents I'm to meet up with. Do I . . . I mean, does Curly know any of them?"

"Only one. The last one. Up in Boston. Jules Crookshank. Washington, Philadelphia, Jersey City, you don't have to worry about."

"You sure?"

She shrugged, and for the first time, I noticed just how fragile she appeared. Why, her shoulders didn't look any wider than the span of my fingers, certainly not wide enough to carry the load that had been dumped on her. "I'm not sure of anything, Jim. About the only thing I would make a bet on now is that in the morning, the sun will rise. Everything else is a toss-up."

I frowned. "You don't give a hombre much room for hope."

Lucy nodded to the Colt resting against my hip. "That's your hope. In the meantime, a couple times a day, you get Weems out here with you. If I need to get you information, I'll show up."

"What about back there, in Atlanta. Did the law get Casement and his boys?"

She nodded. "Yes. Funny thing though, they found Duke and his two top henchmen swimming around in a couple pots of soup in the alley by the train station."

"Is that right?" I grinned.

The door swung open, and George stomped onto

the deck holding a dipper brimming with water. "Here you go, Ma'am."

"Thank you, Mister Weems." Lucy took the dipper, ran a filigreed handkerchief around the rim, then lifted her heavy veil so she could slip the dipper underneath, and drank deeply.

After a few seconds, she returned the dipper to George. "Oh, that was refreshing. Thank you very much, Mr. Weems." Ignoring me, she nodded to George, and then disappeared back into the coach.

George arched an eyebrow. "Mighty fetching little widow there."

"I reckon." I looked out across the Georgia countryside. Beautiful country. Behind us were broad, fertile valleys separated by long, parallel ridges covered with pine and oak and gum. Ahead, to the northeast, tall mountains tickled the bellies of slow-moving clouds. No wonder those Georgia boys fought so hard during the war. Reckon if I'd had me a part of God's handiwork like this, I would of fought hard too.

"Going to be a long ride."

I looked around at George.

"To Washington," he said. "Supposed to get in tomorrow night." He stretched and stared off toward the west. "You reckon that's where South America is?"

"Nope. It's below us, to the south."

"Oh." He stuck his head out so he could see behind the train. "How far do you figure?"

"Beats me. All I know is I'd hate to have to walk it."

George laughed, and we returned to our seats.

Washington was twenty-four hours ahead.

Chapter Fourteen

The drop at Washington went off without a hitch. The train pulled into the station at six forty-five. At eight-thirty, we made the exchange of merchandise, and by nine, we were back on the train heading for Philadelphia.

Our next drop was noon the following day.

"Wish we could go straight on up to Jersey City after this," said George as we walked out of the Philadelphia train station to make our third drop. "I don't cotton to spending the night here. I'd rest a lot easier if we was on the train."

Albert nodded his agreement.

I shrugged. "Whatever you want to do, George. But, our meeting's not scheduled until six o'clock tomorrow evening. We're going to have to hole up somewhere, either here or in Jersey City."

He grimaced. "Reckon you're right." He patted the bulging money belt around his waist. "Still, after this

117

deal, I'd just as soon get out of town. Can't tell. Them old boys might decide to look us up tonight and take back their money.''

''Moving on's fine with me. Albert here can buy our tickets while you and me take care of business. Lorenzo and Miranda can watch the other two suitcases while Albert's busy.''

I kept my fingers crossed that Lucy would spot our change in plans.

She did. When we boarded the train for Jersey City that evening, George elbowed me in the ribs. ''Look there. The little widow. I reckon she's going on up to Jersey City.''

That made sense to me since Jersey City was the next stop. ''Reckon she is, George. Good thinking,'' I replied as we found seats in the coach.

Lorenzo spotted the overhead storage bins running the length of the coach. He grinned. ''Well, I reckon Albert done got us a first-class ride here,'' he said as he slid the suitcases in the bin over our heads. ''Now, we don't have to stumble over them suitcases ever' time we get up.''

With a jerk, a groan, and a strained whistle, the train pulled out. The coach was still crowded, but most folks had settled down for a snooze, so the aisles were fairly clear except for a few hombres who chose to sleep in them.

After a while, George and I were the only ones in our group still awake. I nodded to the rear deck. ''How about some air?''

He grunted and rose to his feet, grimacing against his stiff muscles. ''I'll never complain about no horse again.'' He groaned.

I led the way to the rear. ''Reckon I know what you mean.''

Outside, the fresh air blew away the clogging stuffiness of the coach. I inhaled deeply, remembering those clear nights and that clean air back in Texas. That's where I was heading when I finished this job. Back to Texas.

George broke the silence. "You know something, Curly?"

Reluctantly, I let my dreams slip back into the future. "What?"

He turned to face me and crossed his arms over his chest. "I don't know what it is, but you're different than what you was in Fort Worth."

Every muscle in my body tensed.

"Maybe it's Miranda. I ain't sure, but I want you to know that you've come to feel like kin. You and me, we kinda see things the same way." He chuckled. "I know that sister of mine can be hardheaded, and I reckon I done teased you some about her, but I want you to know, if you and her decide to hitch up, I ain't going to argue it."

His words touched me. Despite his owlhoot trail, where family was concerned, he was a decent man. "Thanks, George. That means a lot to me." And to my own surprise, I realized I was speaking the truth.

The rumble of thunder rolled through the night.

Behind us, the door opened, and Lucy stepped out.

She and George exchanged pleasantries, and within thirty seconds, he disappeared inside for a dipper of water.

"Two drops left," she said. "How you doing?"

"I'm fine. What about you?"

She laid her small hand on my arm. "I'm okay." She paused. "Word is that whoever killed Rozell is with the agency."

For a moment, I stared at her veil, uncomprehending. Then her words registered on me. "You mean . . . that . . . ?"

She glanced back into the car. George was filling the dipper. "Yes. There's a traitor in our organization somewhere. So far, he doesn't know about you. Or, if he does, he hasn't made contact with his own people."

"But, what does that have to do with me?"

"We're not sure. When. . . ."

George opened the door. "Here you are, Ma'am."

Lucy sipped from the dipper and handed it back to George. They chatted for a few minutes, and then she returned to her seat.

"Yep," said George, watching after her. "A mighty fetching young widow."

I nodded, but right then, I didn't have time to think about her comeliness or just how fetching she was. I was trying to figure out who else I had to be on guard against.

Well, I found out a couple minutes later when Miranda pushed through the door and stood between George and me.

"What are you doing out here?" he asked.

She linked her arm through mine. "I just thought Curly and me might get some air."

He winked at me and disappeared inside the car.

Miranda yanked me around. "Curly . . . I mean, Bob. Curly's here. You got to get off the train."

A charge of electricity struck me clean down to my toes. "What?"

"Yeah. I saw him in the next car. He was talking to a couple men." She pushed me away. "Hurry. Get out of here."

I looked off the side of the speeding train at the underbrush blurring past in the night. "And just where should I go?"

"I don't know." The light from the door lit her

face, which was contorted with anguish. "Jump or something."

"I'm not jumping, not at forty miles an hour."

We peered into the car just as Curly pushed through the door at the opposite end of the coach. He came face to face with George, who froze in his tracks. They exchanged puzzled looks, words, and from their elaborate gesticulations, neither one understood what the other was trying to say.

Finally, George pointed toward the end of the car.

I didn't wait for Miranda. I stepped over the knuckle coupler to the next coach and darted inside. There were two coaches and the caboose behind me. Surely, I could find someplace to hide. Of course, as a last resort, I could jump.

Outside the window, a blaze of lightning lit the sky. Moments later, thunder rumbled and crackled. As I exited the coach, I glanced back to see Curly pushing through the crowd. He was going to keep coming, search the entire train.

Without hesitation, I grabbed the ladder and swung around the side of the coach. Quickly, I climbed to the roof of the coach and sprawled beside the walkway, hoping the brakeman in the caboose wouldn't notice me.

The thunder grew louder and lightning cracked. Abruptly, a wall of rain struck the train, soaking me instantly. I grinned to myself. Despite my own discomfort, the blinding rain would prevent the brakeman from spotting me.

If the weather would hold for a spell, maybe Curly would give up and return to the coach with George and Miranda.

I pulled my hat down over my head and pressed up against the walkway, readying myself for a long night.

Suddenly, I remembered Rozell's story about that ritual business and his warning. Don't wash your hair, or it'll fall out. ''Let's see,'' I muttered, grabbing my hat and sticking it under my belly. Let's see if this Indian salve did what it was supposed to do.

I held on tight as the rocking train sped through the rainy night. Despite the time of year, the dog days of summer, the night and the rain combined to send a chill deep into my bones. My teeth chattered, but I remained fixed on that roof, letting the driving rain batter against my head.

After a few minutes, something tickled my nose. I brushed at it, and my fingers touched hair. I felt of my head, and the hair fell out at my touch.

I closed my eyes and lay my head back down on the roof of the coach. My grandchildren, if I lived to have any, would never believe this story. Here I was, chased by outlaws, and what was I doing? Fighting them off? No. Me, I was lying on top of a train in the middle of a thunderstorm waiting for my hair to fall out. That's what I was doing. That would sure be some kind of bedtime story.

Later, as we approached Jersey City, the rain slackened. I could tell from the drops against my head that I was completely bald now. I looked over my shoulder at the caboose. The brakeman in the cupola window of the caboose was still there, but he was reading something. I pulled my hat out from under me and slapped it on my head, but the wind caught it and whipped it away.

Muttering to myself, I gingerly slipped backward on my stomach to the ladder and descended to the deck of the coach. Taking care, I peered through the door window, at the same time removing my checkered vest and throwing it away. No sign of George or Curly.

"Good," I whispered, glancing at the passing buildings as the train slowed. As soon as the train reached the station, I'd hit the ground running, and then worry about my next step.

"Hey, watch it, Baldy. Stop blocking the door," said a guttural voice from behind me. A body brushed me aside as the gruff jasper strode past.

I glanced around, and then ducked my head.

Curly Caruthers!

He had been in the caboose.

I grunted. "Sorry." Immediately, I turned back around as if I was waiting to disembark.

The train continued to slow. Soon, passengers eager to unload crowded on the deck behind me. Keeping my face averted from the coach windows, I waited impatiently. When the train had slowed to a gentle trot, I stepped off and immediately stumbled end over end in the cinders.

Ignoring the cries of alarm from those passengers who had seen me fall, I jumped to my feet and hurried to the station. I wanted to find a good spot to watch for Lucy.

I slouched on a bench in the waiting room. Next to me was a day-old copy of the *Jersey City Evening Journal.* Holding it so I could peer over the top edge, I watched as a flood of weary passengers poured out of the train.

Abruptly, I froze.

Coming into the station were the Weems, followed by Caruthers and the Knott brothers. Miranda's eyes were red. She had been crying, and for a moment, a flare of anger burned my ears.

A dozen steps behind was Lucy.

Faking a limp, I mixed with the passengers until I reached her. "Don't look around. It's me, Jim."

"Stay with me," she whispered harshly. "We got trouble."

Chapter Fifteen

Outside the station, the two families crowded into a single carriage. Lucy hurried to a hansom cab and climbed in. She looked around at me and gasped. "Jim. Is that you?" I couldn't see her face for the veil, but I imagined her eyes bugging out at my bald head.

"What's the matter?" I asked, climbing in beside her. "You never seen a bald man?"

Lucy collected herself enough to order the driver to follow the carriage with the two families. "But, stay far behind them."

I indicated the driver. "Won't he wonder what's going on?"

She removed her hat and veil. "He's one of us."

Somehow, I had the feeling she was going to say that. "You people are just about everywhere, aren't you?"

Lucy glanced at my bald pate. "We try to be. Now, what happened to you?"

Pointing to the carriage, I said. "I guess you noticed Caruthers is with them now."

"Yes." A rueful grin curled her lips. "I thought he was you. When I started talking to him on the train, he acted like I was loco. I guessed something was wrong, but I wasn't sure just what. So, I played dumb and told him I thought he was someone else. Now, I know why he was confused."

"Yeah." I arched an eyebrow. "Now you know, but what's going on with them now? They couldn't have joined up."

"No. The Knott boys held guns on them. Wherever they're going, it's bad news for the Weems."

Her words sent chills up my spine.

The streets were wet from the rain, and the gas lamps gave out only puny glows against the darkness. Three blocks from the station, we pulled to the curb, and Lucy motioned me out. "Get in the carriage behind us."

I did as she said, and the carriage pulled out onto the street after the Weems. "What'd we do that for?" I asked, wondering just why we had swapped our hansom for the carriage.

"We don't want them to know we're following. From time to time, we'll change to a different buggy. A couple more blocks ahead, we've got a donkey cart we'll take. Throws the bad guys off."

"Oh." That was all I could say. I leaned back and closed my eyes. What was the world headed to?

Fifteen minutes later, the Weems' carriage pulled up in front of the Mickey Finn Saloon. Despite the hour being almost four a.m., the saloon was doing a booming business.

"Stop the cart here," Lucy ordered the agent who was disguised as a Mexican peon.

We pulled into the shadows. "See that box at your feet?"

I glanced down. A wooden box sat on the floor of the cart. "What about it?"

"Look inside. There's some disguises. Find something. You and me are going into the saloon." As Lucy spoke, she shed the black dress, turned it inside out to reveal a bright red dress, and slipped back into it.

"Is there anything you people don't think of?" I asked with a mixture of sarcasm and admiration. I pulled out a beard and mustache.

"Not much." She donned a pair of red shoes and stepped from the cart. "Let's go. We walk the rest of the way."

The driver, who had never spoken, said. "I'll wait here for you."

Lucy shook her head. "Take off. I don't know how long we'll be here."

The two families entered the saloon just as Lucy and me reached the corner.

"You got anything definite in mind?" I asked.

"Not yet. Let's just see what's going on."

As we pushed through the batwing doors, we met Cockeye coming out. He didn't look twice at either of us, just brushed past and disappeared into the night.

"Up there," I whispered.

Lucy followed my gaze. On the second floor gallery overlooking the saloon, Curly and the two remaining Knott brothers ushered the Weems family through an open door.

I took Lucy's elbow. "Let's get a table over in the corner."

The saloon was loud and lusty, bellowing with shouts, curses, songs, and laughter, with a festive merriment thicker than the smoke filling the room.

I bellied up to the bar and ordered two mugs of beer. I looked into the mirror behind the bartender and froze. I didn't recognize myself in the black beard and mustache beneath a head shiny as a snooker ball.

Within an hour, the crowd thinned, and two swampers emerged from the back room and ran wet mops over the floors, emptied brass spittoons, and slid chairs back under the tables, readying the Mickey Finn for the next shift of merrymakers.

No one had entered or left the upstairs room.

"What are we going to do now?"

Lucy shrugged. "Play it by ear, I guess." Her eyebrows knit in a frown. "How did the Knott boys get involved in this? You got any idea?"

"Yeah. You're looking at how they got involved."

Her frown deepened, and I explained how the Knott brothers had waylaid me outside of San Antone. "At the time, I figured it didn't make much difference because I was bailing out of this mess, but Rozell caught me with a short loop."

A wry grin flickered across her lips. "He tossed a bunch of short loops."

I returned her grin. "Well, he sure caught me with one." I went on to tell her about our scheme to delay the Knott boys.

At six, Cockeye returned just as the next surge of patrons stormed the bar.

At seven, I pushed my hot, unfinished beer aside. "The drop isn't until six tonight. Why don't you grab some sleep? I'll keep an eye peeled."

She gave me a weary smile. "Across the street is a boardinghouse, Ma Baley's. Second floor, second door on the right. I'll be back about noon."

* * *

Later, Cockeye left the room and returned minutes later with a sack strung over his shoulder and a pail of beer swinging from his hand. It looked like Curly and the Knott brothers planned on keeping everyone inside until the drop.

I was right. Not once during the morning did they leave the room.

Just before Lucy returned, a stranger wearing a black bowler, a short cloak over a gray suit, and white spats climbed the stairs and knocked on the door. I sat forward and studied him. There was something familiar about the man, but before I could pin it down, the door opened, and he stepped inside.

A few minutes later, he left, but instead of descending the stairs, he paused and stared out over the saloon. Other than a pointy nose, there was nothing unusual about him, just a plain-looking hombre. After a moment, he disappeared down a second-floor hallway. I tugged at my fake mustache. I had the feeling I'd seen that jasper before, but for the life of me, I couldn't remember when or where.

A few minutes later, Lucy relieved me. I told her about the stranger before I headed for Ma Baley's and some much-needed sleep.

"They're still up there. Someone doesn't want to take any chances," Lucy whispered when I returned from my nap.

"What about the stranger I mentioned?"

She arched an eyebrow. "No sign of him either."

I wondered just who that jasper was. "What are we going to do when they leave? Follow them?"

Lucy leaned her elbows on the table and looked up at me. "That's all we can do." She turned her gaze back to the room. "They're not going to hurt anyone unless they're forced to."

I clucked my tongue, thinking of hardheaded Albert or the unpredictable George Weems. "Just keep your heads, boys," I muttered.

"What did you say?" Lucy looked around at me.

"Nothing. Just talking to myself."

At five o'clock, I felt Lucy stiffen by my side.

I looked up just as the door opened and Cockeye stepped out on the gallery overlooking the saloon, followed by the Weems family, then Leadbelly and Bighead, and finally Curly Caruthers.

Who knows how the fight started? A saloon filled with smoke thicker than a California fog, everybody drunk or well on the way to that state, heated words exchanged, tempers flared, and fists flew.

As the two families descended the stairs, the subdued buzz of the saloon exploded into a firestorm of fists, teeth, and feet. A bottle of whiskey smashed against the wall by my head. Immediately a limp body followed the bottle, and both sagged to the floor in broken heaps.

"Duck," I yelled, a command wasted on Lucy for she was already under the table, clenching the neck of a whiskey bottle like a club.

I dropped to her side and peered from under the table through the flying bottles, bodies, and chairs. The Knotts and Weems were caught up in the melee halfway down the stairs. Curly stood in front like a giant of old, throwing off drunken men like rag dolls.

The three Knott brothers, guns drawn, stood behind Miranda and her brothers. Curly glanced back at them and with a wave of his arm charged into the boiling battle, knocking drunken gladiators aside as he opened a path to the door.

Leadbelly jammed his six-gun in George's back and shoved the redheaded outlaw after Curly. As one, the small entourage moved forward.

A poker table sailed from out of the smoke and bounced off Lorenzo's shoulder and head, sending him spinning into the brawl. Leadbelly yelled at Lorenzo, but the young man was sucked into the fray like quicksand. Leadbelly shook his head and turned back to the others.

Once or twice, I spotted Lorenzo's dark hair as he was battered from pillar to post, but I had to give him credit. He seemed to be handing out almost as much as he was getting. The problem was he could fight in only one direction at a time, and fists and boots were coming from every corner of the compass.

The rest of the family was lost in the swirling crowd that rolled over a snooker table and poured through the batwing doors onto the street.

Lorenzo's head snapped back, and he stumbled sideways.

I had to shout to be heard over the noise. ''He's coming this way.''

Staggering like a drunk, Lorenzo walked into a pile-driver fist that lifted him into the air and sent him skittering across the snooker table on his back.

For a moment, I toyed with the notion of going to his aid, but when a chair was smashed against the table under which were crouched, I decided discretion was the better part of valor and remained huddled beside Lucy. I told myself that I didn't want to leave her alone. A woman in a place like this.

Suddenly, a pug-nosed, gap-toothed face appeared under the table, leering at us. "Well, well, well, look who we got here. We. . . . "

Lucy smashed the whiskey bottle across his face, and he dropped to the floor like a poleaxed steer.

Through a gap in the battle, we spotted Lorenzo as he rolled off the snooker table and smashed facedown on the floor. Slowly, he pushed himself to his feet and stumbled unseeing toward us.

A fist caught him in the jaw, sending him staggering in another direction.

"You better go get him," Lucy yelled.

A fist got him first, turning him in another direction. "Just hold on a second," I shouted. "He'll be coming back this way in a minute."

Sure enough, a couple more fists and a whiskey bottle over the head sent Lorenzo reeling toward us.

Lucy nodded to a door behind us. "That goes to the alley."

We jumped to our feet and grabbed Lorenzo, hustling him to the rear door. I yanked on it. It refused to budge. "What the blazes . . . it's locked. We've got to find some. . . . "

"Yaaaaaa!"

I jerked around just in time to see a wild-eyed, grinning drunk duck his head and charge us. I sidestepped and grabbed his belt and propelled him into the door. His hard head punched a round hole in the door, and his broad shoulders tore it from the jamb. His momentum carried him into the alley.

I looked at Lucy and shrugged. "That's one way to get it open."

We stepped over the unconscious man whose head was still stuck in the door.

The screaming, shouting revelers found the open

door and spilled into the alley, but Lucy and I had already disappeared around the corner with Lorenzo.

Five minutes later, we laid him across the bed at Ma Baley's Boarding House.

Hanging in the closet was a fresh change of apparel for each of us.

Chapter Sixteen

"I don't like the idea of just tagging after them," I muttered as I looked at myself in the mirror. The four-button suit the Secret Service provided me was almost too small. "We need to do something. We should have at least followed them to the drop." The hem of the coat fit too snug over my six-gun, so I unfastened the two bottom buttons. Then I placed the black bowler on my head.

Lucy said. "I told you. Our agents are watching them. You and me, we've got to be ready to follow them on the train to Boston."

The slender blond had exchanged her red dress for a very demure gray travel outfit. The skirt was full, the jacket was full, the cape was full. She lifted the left side of her jacket to reveal a hidden derringer.

"That oughta take care of you," I said, chuckling.

She patted the outside of her thigh. "If it

doesn't, this one will.'' A grin spread across her face when she saw the surprise on my own. ''And if that doesn't . . . '' She left the remainder of the sentence unfinished as she raised the right side of her jacket.

I whistled softly. ''You people are dead serious, aren't you?''

''Five hundred percent.''

''What about him?'' I hooked my thumb at Lorenzo.

''Leave him. My people will send someone by later to pick him up.'' She tucked her blond hair under her hat.

On the way to the train station, Lucy explained that agents would tail the gang even after the drop, never losing sight of them. ''You and me, we'll be aboard the seven forty-five to Boston, waiting for Caruthers and his bunch. If for some reason they miss the train, we'll be notified.''

I started to mention the stranger again, but shrugged it off. He couldn't be that important anyway, or Lucy would have said something. Still, he reminded me of someone.

Outside the station, she paused to study me. A becoming smile played over her lips. She removed my hat. ''You know, for a bald-headed man, you're not bad looking.'' She reached up and straightened the beard and mustache. ''You need to watch this. I'm not too keen on that newfangled paste that holds the beard on.''

''Don't worry. It's held tight since yesterday, even through the brawl in the saloon.'' I took the bowler from her and stuck it back on my head. ''Let's get settled where we can keep an eye on the station.''

In addition to its daily linkup of a Pullman, three

day coaches, and a baggage car, the seven forty-five to Boston also hauled Buffalo Bill's Wild West Show, a contingent consisting of an additional day coach, a stock car, and two flatcars carrying the animals and tents for the show in Boston.

After Lucy and me found a seat on the coach from where we could watch the main gate, I said, "What I don't understand is why we just can't arrest them now. Why do we have to wait for Boston?"

"I told you." When she saw the puzzled frown on my face, she added. "Or at least I thought I told you. We ... maybe I should say Rozell thought that the kingpin in Boston, Jules Crookshank, controls everything down to Jersey City, especially the counterfeiting markets. That's what got this whole plan going. If that's true, and if we can catch him with the evidence, we'll have taken a long step in getting control of our currency back. Stick him in prison for twenty years, and maybe we'll have a chance to smash his gang."

"Yeah. I remember now. You said Rozell was looking for a promotion."

"That's it." She hesitated. Her face grew thoughtful. "It's not too late for you to bow out. You've done what you're supposed to. I can vouch for that."

Now, I'd be lying if I didn't say her offer was mighty tempting, but I'd come to like this woman sitting next to me, and as strange as it might seem, I didn't want anything to happen to Miranda or her brothers.

These feelings were strange to me, for the only hombre I'd ever had much to do with was Larimer H. Harrison, the old gambler who had taken me in and raised me, and even then it was pretty much a rough-and-tumble, take-care-of-yourself existence.

So, when these new tingly feelings ran up my arms, I wasn't sure just what to do about them, except hang around.

I grinned at her. "Reckon you're right, but I'll just tag along. Keep you safe. After all, like you say, you're the only one who knows the deal Rozell made me."

She returned my smile, and for the first time I could remember, a warm glow of satisfaction flowed through my veins. It was almost like I had finally found someplace where I belonged.

Suddenly, Lucy stiffened. Her dark eyes, which only moments before had been warm and laughing, turned icy.

I looked around. With Caruthers leading the way, the entourage passed through the main gate and cut across the loading platform to the first coach.

As prearranged, I moved to the seat ahead of Lucy. We didn't want them to know we were traveling together.

"Get ready," Lucy whispered as Curly pushed through the door.

It was like looking in a mirror. He and I could have been identical twins. Quickly, I looked out the window, keeping my face averted as they made their way down the coach and took two sets of seats across the aisle from us. I felt eyes on me. Had they recognized me? I tried to ignore them, but the feeling persisted.

Very casually, I removed my hat, revealing my bald head.

Right on time, the train pulled out on the last leg of our journey. By this time tomorrow, everything would be settled. I looked around the coach. At the far end sat some of the performers of Buffalo Bill's Wild West Show, cowpokes, a couple Indians, even one jasper who looked like he was from some foreign country.

The monotonous clacking of the wheels soon droned me to sleep.

When I awakened some time later, Lucy was sleeping. I eased out of my seat and, rubbing my eyes, made my way to the water barrel where I filled a dipper and drank deeply.

I looked outside. The dark night and the dim light in the coach combined to fashion a mirror out of the window. I froze when I saw myself. My mustache was missing.

Instantly, my hand went to my face.

"This what you're looking for, pardner?"

I spun and stared into the beady eyes of Leadbelly Knott. He wore a smirk across his fat lips. At the other end of the coach, all the others, the Weems and Knotts, were looking on.

Before I could reply, Leadbelly yanked my beard off and stared at me. "I thought you looked familiar." He half turned his head and shouted over his shoulder. "Hey, Curly. This here's the hombre who . . ."

Those were the last words he uttered. I swung from the floor, catching him on the point of the chin and knocking him into some sleeping travelers. For whatever insane reason, I grabbed the beard from him as he fell.

I threw one last look at Curly, who was charging toward me. Just before I yanked open the door, I noticed that Lucy had vanished.

By now, the commotion had brought several passengers to their feet. They stumbled into the aisle, blocking Curly, who cursed and shoved them aside.

In the next coach, I found the conductor. "Quick. There's a man in the next car causing trouble. He's already beat some poor man in the head."

With a loud curse, the conductor rushed out in one direction, and I rushed in the other, anxious to find someplace where I could hide for the next few hours. I crossed my fingers for Lucy, hoping she'd found a secure hideout.

The next coach was one of those new Pullmans where seats fold into beds and heavy curtains are pulled for privacy. My first thought was to find an empty berth, but I knew Curly and the Knott brothers would check every one of them.

Then a devious idea struck me. Near the end of the Pullman, I laid the beard on the floor in front of a berth. Then I ducked outside the door and waited in the darkness, far enough back so the dim light from the coach wouldn't illumine me.

Just as I planned, Curly and Cockeye skidded to a halt by the beard and drew their six-guns. Curly yanked the curtain back and both men stepped forward.

Well, sir, the scream of that terrified fat lady could be heard above the whistle of our engine. It was louder, longer, and shriller than any train whistle I ever heard, in this life or the next.

Curly and Cockeye stumbled back and tumbled through the drawn curtains of the booth behind them.

More screams, and within seconds, the entire pullman was awash with half-dressed females swinging whatever kind of weapon they could get their hands on at the two hapless outlaws.

Grinning to myself, I shinnied up the ladder to the walkway on top of the coach and, dropping into a crouch, hurried back down the train to the last day coach, the one Lucy and me had been in. Behind the coach were the two flatcars loaded down with a jumble of tents and poles, stacked on, over, and under wagons and coaches of every description.

I dropped to my stomach as I approached the end of the car. For several minutes, I lay motionless, studying the dark shadows spilling across the flatcars. A shadow emerged from the stagecoach on one of the flatcars. I pressed my lanky body closer to the roof of the car. The shadow came closer, then disappeared. I remained motionless. Moments later, the shadow appeared in the second flatcar, moving away from me.

Slowly, I climbed down and peered through the rear window of the day coach.

Everyone in the coach had clustered around the door at the opposite end of the car, their backs to me.

Suddenly, a familiar voice cursed in the darkness behind me. Bighead! I looked around frantically. If I scampered back up on top, he might spot me. I didn't have a choice.

Moving quickly, I slipped inside.

I was trapped!

Then I noticed the storage area along either side of the ceiling, a series of enclosed compartments extending the length of the car above the seats.

Without hesitation, I swung into the first compartment, the one above the seats in which Lucy and I had sat. There were a couple suitcases in the cubicle, so I slid them to the front and lay down behind them, taking care to lie across the supports. The bottom of the compartment was covered with thin strips of lapstrake, none strong enough to support a hundred and eighty pounds, but if I spread my weight, I figured it could hold me.

I was wrong. Even the compartment supports groaned, not having been constructed for such a weight. And the rocking of the train added to the strain. I decided I'd better find another cubbyhole.

Before I could move, the back door of the coach opened, and then I heard Leadbelly's voice. "Bighead. Where you been? You seen anything of that jasper?"

In his drawling monotone, Bighead replied. "Nope. Nary a hair."

Leadbelly muttered a curse. "Sit down. Don't know where Curly or your brother is. Still lookin' for that other feller, I reckon."

They sat directly under me. I dared not move.

Soon, Curly and Cockeye joined them.

Leadbelly was the first to speak. "You find him?"

"Nope," said Curly in his gravelly voice. "That low-down skunk disappeared like a ghost. Couldn't find a trace of him."

There was a short pause. Then Leadbelly spoke again, this time to Cockeye. "What happened to you? Looks like someone whopped you up alongside your head."

Cockeye mumbled some excuse I couldn't make out. If I hadn't been four feet over their heads, I would've laughed. The picture of those women lambasting Curly and Cockeye was too comical to resist.

A guttural voice spoke up. "What about the Weems?"

Leadbelly replied. "What about them, Bighead?"

"Yeah. They still tied up in the stagecoach, good and snug. I just come back in from out there."

I felt something touch my boot. I tried to take a

look, but I couldn't crane my neck enough to see anything. I felt it again, a faint tap.

The rocking train hit a sharp curve, and the luggage shifted into me, pushing me against the wall. A support cracked. I stiffened and remained as still as I could, expecting the entire compartment to collapse.

But it held. I sighed with relief.

Then I felt the tapping against my boot again. What the Sam Hill could that be?

A booming voice answered the question for me.

"Say, Pards," said the voice. "Sorry to bother you, but I'm with the Buffalo Bill show down there. Seems like one of our performers from India has done gone and lost some of his gear."

Curly replied, his tone surly. "We ain't seen nothing of it."

Cockeye spoke up. "You say India? Whereabouts is that?"

"Beats me," replied the cowboy. "Across the ocean somewhere."

"What is it? What'd he lose?" asked Cockeye.

The booming voice chuckled. "You'll know when you see it. The hombre's a snake charmer. He's lost a couple of his snakes."

At that moment, something tapped my boot again, and I exploded.

Suitcases flew out.

The compartment collapsed right on top of Curly and the Knott brothers.

I burst out kicking and stomping. "Snake! Snake! Snake!"

Everyone jumped to their feet and began stomping. I glanced up at the pieces of the compartment dangling from the ceiling.

In the next compartment, just about where my

foot was, lay a coil of rope, one end loose and bobbing up and down with each rocking motion of the train.

Without hesitation, I spun Bighead around and shoved him into the others, sending them all sprawling on the floor.

I darted out the back door, and once again swung up for the all too familiar walkway along the top of the coach. I made my way forward, not sure just what I was going to do. I needed to find Lucy!

Chapter Seventeen

Lucy found me.

I had planned to hide out by the coal tender, but as I leaped from the roof of the Pullman to the baggage car, Lucy called to me from below.

Quickly, I climbed down.

She grabbed my hand and yanked me into the Pullman. "Come on."

I didn't argue.

Inside, she pulled back the curtains in the first berth. "Hurry. Get in next to the wall."

"No." I shook my head. "This'll be the first place they search."

She smiled. "Don't worry. Just do what I say."

So, I climbed in and pressed up against the window. Lucy leaned in and threw a blanket over me. Then I felt her climb in. She whispered. "They search here, all they'll find is me."

When I heard the curtains close, I threw the blanket

off my head and propped myself up on my elbow. The berth was dark, but moonlight poured through the window, bathing us with a cool, bluish glow. She was undoing her hair, letting it spill over her shoulders.

I spoke softly. "Don't you figure they'll recognize you?"

She shook her head. "They'll never connect us. We weren't even sitting together."

"What if they want to know why you disappeared from the coach when the fracas started?"

Her smile broadened. Innocently, she replied, "Me? I'm just a helpless woman who is frightened of violence. I fled the car so I wouldn't be harmed."

I lay back and grinned. Caruthers and his cohorts didn't stand a chance against this woman.

Lucy lay back, and we stared at the bottom of the berth over our heads.

I whispered. "I know where the Weems are. Leadbelly has them tied up in one of the stage coaches of the flatcar. He'll leave them there until they get ready for the drop. You're going to need quite a few agents to cover everything."

She grunted. "Yeah, but what if only two or three went to the drop? What if somehow, we could keep the rest here. Or at least in a hotel somewhere," she added.

"That's it," I exclaimed, sitting up too fast. I banged my head against the top berth.

A muffled voice from above said. "Will you please go to sleep and stop talking."

Lucy ducked her head and blushed.

I grinned and whispered. "Now, listen. Here's what we'll do."

Within a few minutes, we laid our plans, nothing elaborate, but if they worked, we could tie the entire operation up in a neat package for the Secret Service.

Things went wrong from the beginning, at least on my end.

An hour later, while the sky was still dark, I slipped from the berth and made my way over the rooftops to the flatcar on which the stagecoach was lashed. The plan was for me to follow Miranda and her brothers to wherever Curly took them. Then, after Curly left for the drop, I'd contact the Secret Service. Simple.

Except when I climbed down off the roof, Cockeye, six-gun in hand, was standing in the doorway. A lantern lit his leering grin. He stared at me and the passing scenery. "Well, well, well. Lookie here who we got." He cocked the hammer. "It ain't good manners to try to fool people, Mister Whoever-You-Might-Be. Some folks don't cotton to that kind of misbehavin' and might just decide to do something about it."

I thought fast. "Better ease up on that trigger, Cockeye." I nodded behind him. "Curly won't like you boys calling attention to yourself."

"Huh?" He glanced over his shoulder.

That was all the time I needed. I swung from the ground and whopped him alongside the head. He spun around and crashed into the door.

I leaped for the flatcar. Just as I landed, someone stepped out of the stagecoach. Bighead! We both froze, then with a shout like the growl of a grizzly bear, he charged.

Behind me came a shout from Cockeye.

Two to one. I didn't like those odds at all so I leaped under a nearby buckboard and crawled behind a pile of canvas. The sky was dark, and in among all the equipment, it was even darker.

Knowing the brothers would follow, I slipped under a rack of tent poles and found myself beneath a canvas with a pile of saddles.

I grinned to myself. I was in a warren of Wild West equipment, with narrow tunnels and passages criss-crossing the flatcar.

"Over there," yelled Cockeye. "Get over there. I'm going after him."

Crawling as fast as I could, I discovered boxes stacked in several rows and tiers in one corner of the flatcar. Feeling my way along, I found that narrow walkways separated the stacks, ending at the edge of the flatcar.

To the east, false dawn lit the sky, and slowly objects began to take shape.

An idea popped into my head. "Yeah," I muttered. "In this light, a jasper could just walk off the edge of the car if he wasn't careful." I inspected the boxes along the edge of the flatcar for handholds. Heavy ropes lashed them to the car. "Why not?" I chuckled.

Backtracking, I looked around for either of the brothers. Suddenly, Cockeye's head popped up over a buckboard seat. We saw each other at the same time. He rushed toward me, and I turned and raced down the narrow corridor to the edge of the car.

At the end of the walkway, I grabbed one of the ropes and swung around the corner. The train was approaching a bridge over a wide river.

"Now I got you," shouted Cockeye, his voice bursting with anticipation.

With the wind whipping at me, I clung to the side of the boxes, holding to the heavy ropes for dear life when Cockeye went rushing past.

When he realized that nothing was under his feet except air, he froze, one arm extended to the front, one arm extended to the back, one leg extended to the front, one to the back. He maintained that graceful posture as he arched off the flatcar and over the edge of the bridge. The last I saw of him, he was headed straight down, holding himself in that same stately bearing.

Climbing back onto the flatcar, I made my way toward the stagecoach. Now, there was only three owl-hoots left, Curly, Leadbelly, and Bighead. If I could free Miranda and her brothers, maybe we could call a truce long enough for them to give me a hand.

I crouched under the buckboard. The stagecoach was less than twenty feet from me, but by now, the sun had risen. I had to be careful. Slowly, I stuck my head out, and when I did, it exploded with a thousand stars.

A sharp throbbing pain lanced through my skull, pushing aside the darkness, forcing me to awaken. I tried to open my eyes, but the bright morning sun drove searing rivets into my skull.

Rough hands yanked me to my feet. "Get up, whatever your name is."

I stumbled to my feet. My head felt like wild horses were trying to kick their way out. I swayed on my feet. Hands pushed me forward. When I finally got my eyes open, I saw Miranda and her brothers standing on the ground beside the flatcar.

A gun muzzle jammed me in the back. "Climb down, and fast," growled Leadbelly. "Or I'll blow a hole in you big enough to drive a wagon through."

I stumbled down off the flatcar and staggered after the others to a carriage. Despite the pounding in my skull, I tried to keep up with our route, but I must've passed out once or twice, for I lost all track of time.

Dimly, I was aware we were meandering through Boston. Probably Curly planned on stashing us somewhere while he made the drop. In the background, insistent voices jabbed at me, but I was too weary to force myself from the stupor enveloping me. Finally, the voices went away.

I didn't remember a thing until around noon when I awakened. My head still throbbed, but it was bearable. I must've been carried inside for I was laying on the floor, staring at a mouse hole in the wall. I turned my head.

Across the plain room, George and Albert were sitting in ladder-back chairs, glaring at me, but Miranda smiled from where she was seated on the bed.

I struggled to sit up. "Where's Curly?" I asked her.

George spoke for his sister. "They're in the next room."

Albert interrupted. "Why? You gonna try to trick them like you did us? You know, it's your fault we're in this mess. Lorenzo's gone. Dead probably. If it hadn't been for you, none of this. . . ."

"Shut up, Albert. In our kind of business, that's expected," said George, keeping his voice soft. "It ain't no more this feller's fault than yours." He arched a red eyebrow. His voice took a hard edge. "I just want to know what you was up to, Mister Smith . . . if that's even your name. You suckered us, suckered us good."

I stood up, rolling my head on my neck in an effort to work out some of the kinks. I grinned weakly at Miranda. No sense in telling more lies. "My name isn't Smith, it's Jim Wells, and I reckon you're entitled to the truth, but first, I can tell you Lorenzo is okay. He's back in Jersey City, with the law."

"Thank the Lord," muttered Miranda.

George and Albert relaxed noticeably.

Then I told them my story, from beginning to the present, all about the Secret Service, the spying, everything.

When I finished, George shook his head and gave me a wry grin. "Yep, Mister Wells, it shore looks like you done gone and suckered ever'body, yourself included.''

Our eyes met. ''I can't blame you folks for hating me, George. But I got to tell you the truth. After I got to know you and your sister, I despised myself for what I was doing. You might be on the wrong side of the law, but to me, you're good people.''

George nodded. ''Thanks, Mister Wells. Them's nice words.''

Albert snorted. ''Bull. . . . ''

George backhanded him, knocking him out of his chair.

George grinned shyly. ''And I . . . '' He glanced at Miranda. ''I mean, we took a liking to you. Lorenzo too.'' He nodded to his brother on the floor. ''Albert's always been ornery, ever' since he was just a grass-hopper.''

I hooked my thumb at the closed door. ''Looks like Caruthers showed up at the wrong time, huh?''

''Yep.'' George winced. ''Busted out of jail and just happened to run into Leadbelly at our place.''

Albert climbed to his feet and retired across the room, glaring at his brother sullenly.

I suppressed a grin. ''How'd they find us?''

A crooked grin played over his square face. He pointed to his mop of red hair. ''Wasn't hard. Dallas was the closest rail line, and you can't hide four heads of red hair like we got. They just tracked us from there.''

''Are you all right?'' I asked Miranda.

''Yes.'' Her rugged face blushed.

''They haven't hurt you?''

''No.''

''Good.'' I turned back to George. ''We've got to get outta here. You know they're not going to turn us loose when this is all over.''

Albert broke out of his sullen mood. "That ain't what they said. They said once they made the drop, they'd set us loose."

I shook my head. "What would you expect them to say, Albert? You think they'd admit they're going to kill you? No. They want us to sit here like nice, well-behaved little schoolchildren until they get back. They can't afford to let us live. We know too much."

Without giving Albert or George a chance to reply, I continued. "If we can just get out of here, we're okay. The law is waiting for Curly and the others at the drop."

George and Miranda shot a startled look at each other, then he turned back to me. "Curly changed the drop."

My mouth dropped open.

George continued. "From what I overheard, somebody on the inside got word to him that the law was planning a trap."

On the inside! My jaw couldn't drop any more. I just stood there like a dummy trying to trap flies with my mouth. Finally, I managed to put together an intelligent remark. "What?"

He nodded. "That's right. Curly thought I was asleep when he told Leadbelly that he had a partner on the inside of this Secret Service thing you was talking about. The partner was the one who passed word on to Curly about the trap."

His words hit me in my stomach like the kick of a wide-eyed bronc. Lucy? Immediately, I dismissed the idea. But who? Rozell was dead. Only the three of us knew about the scheme.

Then I remembered the man in the shadows back at the jail, the one who told Rozell to give me five thousand instead of two. Slowly I nodded as all the pieces fell together.

The hombre back in the jail had to be the same one I spotted knocking on the upstairs door in the Mickey Finn Saloon. He was Rozell's boss.

I shook my head. "Sure, why not?" I muttered, more to myself than George and the others. "Simple. So blasted simple."

"What?" George rose from his chair. "What's simple?"

"Huh?" I realized George was talking to me. "Oh. I just figured out who's behind this. Not his name. I don't know that, but I know who he is."

I went on to explain that, as Rozell's boss, this jasper was in a position to know everything that was taking place. I had informed my contact who passed the word on to Rozell, who in turn passed the information to his boss.

George whistled softly. "That feller was gettin' everyone else to do his work, and then at the end, he just steps in and rakes off the profit."

"That's just about it," I replied. "And that's another reason they'll have to kill us. This guy doesn't want anyone to know he's with the Secret Service. He'll take his profit, probably stay with the agency another year or so, and then retire." I hesitated, then added. "And no one will be the wiser. I. . . . "

Suddenly, I stiffened.

George took a step toward me. "What's wrong?"

"Lucy."

"Who's Lucy?" Miranda asked.

"My contact in Bandera. She's here in Boston, and she knows just about as much as we do. That means. . . . "

Albert finished the sentence for me. "They'll have to kill her too."

I looked at him. The sullen anger had fled his face.

He nodded. "You're dead right, Mister Wells. We got to get out of here and get this mess straightened out."

"Jim. My name's Jim." I grinned at him.

"How do you figure we get out of this place?" George pointed to the window. "We're on the third floor."

"The bed. Tie the sheets and blankets together, and we shinny down. We'll go to the drop and bring the law back." I peered out the window. "There's buildings up and down the street. Albert and Miranda can hide in one of them and keep watch on this place while George and me go to the drop and get the law."

Miranda spoke up. "What if Curly leaves before you two get back?"

I shrugged. "I hope he doesn't."

George cleared his throat. "You go by yourself, Jim." He nodded to Albert and Miranda. "If Curly leaves, we'll follow. Leave signs for you. If the trail takes an unlikely turn, one of us will hang back." A grin slid across his square face. "I reckon it'll be quite a change to be the posse this time instead of the outlaw."

"I reckon," I replied, returning his smile.

We jammed a chair under the doorknob and tore the sheets and blankets off the bed. Five minutes later, we were scampering across the street and down an alley.

Chapter Eighteen

Finding Lucy and the squad of agents was easy. I took a cab down to Commercial Street and stepped out in front of the Boston Bay Tavern to look around.

Immediately, Lucy hailed me. "What do you think you're doing?" she shouted. "You've ruined our trap."

Hastily, I began to explain the switch in plans, but then I paused and studied the faces looking at me. The man I had spotted back in the saloon was not present. I continued.

"But how did they find out?" Lucy asked when I finished.

I pulled her toward the cab. "I'll tell you on the way. Let's go. Curly might have already left."

Five minutes later, we were racing back into the Back Bay District. During the ride, I laid out my theory to Lucy and the four other agents.

A frown knitted her forehead. "You think Rozell's superior is the one behind it all?"

"That's the only explanation I see. How could he know all these details? Only you and Rozell knew. He had to pass it on to his boss."

One of the agents said, "Who else was in on this, Lucy?"

"I don't know. Rozell gave me my orders."

"Who gave Rozell his?"

Another agent answered. "He took his orders from Bordworther."

"There's asking a lot for us to believe, mister," said yet another agent.

I returned his cold stare. "I'm not asking you to believe a thing. I'm telling you what I saw and what I figured. I'm no Secret Service man like you boys. You got a better idea, I'm all for it."

Lucy asked. "Can you describe the man you saw, Jim?"

"Hard to. Nothing unusual I saw, except he had a pointy little nose. That was about all I. . . . "

As one, they stiffened and sat back in the cab. The look on their faces told me I'd dropped a sack of wildcats right in the middle of their little party.

Lucy took a deep breath. "Are you sure, Jim? Really sure?"

I nodded emphatically. "Yeah. Skinny jasper. Wore one of those bowler type hats and cape of sorts that hung almost to the floor. But his nose was pointed . . . just like the tip of a cow horn. Oh, yeah, he wore spats too."

"Why didn't you tell me about his nose back in Jersey City?"

"I didn't figure it was that important."

For the next few blocks, we rode in silence. Nobody had bothered to put a name to Pointy Nose, but from the way they were carrying on, I figured I'd guessed right. I broke the silence. "So you know this jasper, huh?"

Lucy nodded. "Francis Bordworther, Deputy Associate Agent for the Southwestern Region." She hesitated and looked at each of her comrades for help. They dropped their eyes. She turned back to me. "I can't believe it. Not Bordworther. Why, he's a regular visitor to President Hayes."

"Maybe I'm talking about another hombre. I don't reckon this Bordworther is the only one with a pointy nose."

We rounded the corner onto Front Street. I leaned out the window and yelled at the driver. "Over there. Stop at that alley."

Miranda spotted us and lumbered into the street.

"Great galloping galoshes," muttered one of the agents looking over my shoulder. "What is that?"

I looked at him and spoke deliberately. "That . . . is a lady, mister. Don't you forget it."

The cab jerked to a halt, and I threw open the door.

Miranda stared up at us, her red hair looking more and more like a pile of mussed-up hay. She pointed down the street. "They went thataway." She nodded across the street where an angry man was waving his hands at one of the local police. "George and Albert stole that man's horse so they could follow."

One of the agents groaned.

I ignored him. "Get in." I pulled her into the already crowded cab. "What kind of sign are they going to leave for us?"

Miranda wedged her ample bottom in between two agents, nearly filling the cab to overflowing. "They just said we'd know."

"That could mean anything." I thought for a moment. "I'm climbing up with the driver. The rest of you hang out the windows. Look for anything odd at a corner. No telling what those old boys will do, but one thing's for sure, they'll leave some kind of mark pointing their way.''

I swung out the window and climbed up with the driver, a crusty old man who yelled, "You ain't allowed up here. Only me."

With a grunt, I plopped down beside him and laid my hand on my six-gun. "I'm either up here with you, or I'm up here all alone. It don't make me no difference."

He studied me a moment, then shrugged. "I allus like to have good company." He flicked the reins against the horse's rump. "Let's go, Ben."

We traveled straight for several blocks, and I began to worry. What if we'd already missed a turn? A shout came from below. "Stop. Back up. Head down that last street."

The old driver deftly whipped the cab around and turned down the last intersection. I grinned. Now I knew what kind of sign George and Albert would leave. A cluster of men and women were staring at several broken windows in a dry goods store.

We pulled up beside them. "What's going on?" I shouted.

The store owner glared up at me. "Two redheaded idiots on horse rode up the sidewalk and kicked my windows out. That's what happened. You the law?"

"No." I hooked my thumb over my shoulder. "They're coming." I elbowed the driver. "Let's go."

Well, I got to admit, George and Albert left a mighty plain trail. Even a blind man could've followed it. Why, they broke so many windows along the way, they'd have to spend five years at hard labor just to pay for them all.

"Looks like they're heading to the North End District," Lucy yelled from below.

Twenty minutes later at a broken window, we pulled up.

I leaned over the side of the carriage and shouted at Lucy. "Up ahead. There's our boys."

A couple blocks up the street, George stepped out from behind a brick building and waved us forward.

He grinned when we reached him. "About time. They've already started the dance."

"Where?"

He nodded down an alley. "A warehouse on the next street. At the dock. Albert's watching."

We bailed out of the cab and followed George, but not before I noticed one of the agents help Miranda from the cab.

Constructed of red brick, the warehouse covered several blocks along the wharf. Beyond the long, low building, schooners lay in dock, their tall masts towering above the warehouse.

Albert looked around. "Curly and the Knott boys just went in. They had a stranger with them."

Lucy took charge. "What'd he look like?"

Albert glared at her.

George bellowed. "Answer her."

Sullenly, Albert replied. "Skinny. Wore one of them round hats and something funny on his feet."

"Bordworther!" Lucy glanced at me, then turned back to her agents. Quickly, she made the assignments, placing three along the dock and one in the front. She nodded to me. "You and me will go in from the front."

"What about us?" George growled.

"Yeah." Albert chimed in. "We didn't come all this way to miss the fun."

Lucy frowned at me. I shrugged. "I'd take them

anytime. You take your boys around back. George, Albert, and me will go in the front.''

''I'll go with William,'' said Miranda, stepping to the side of the agent who had helped her from the cab.

For a moment, no one spoke. Stunned, I stared at Miranda.

William colored. He glanced at Lucy uncomfortably. ''Uh, no. No, Miranda. Maybe it's best you stay here out of danger.''

Miranda replied in her most feminine manner she could muster. ''Bull! Ain't nobody gonna keep me from goin' with you, William.'' She glared at Lucy. ''Nobody!''

I resisted a grin. ''She means it.''

Lucy shrugged. ''Let's go then.''

Five-hundred-pound bales of cotton filled the dark warehouse, lining corridors that crisscrossed other corridors. The cart-wide aisles seemed to stretch for miles, and the musty air was laced with the tang of salt. A series of catwalks spanned the rafters. I felt just like one of those little red ducks in a shooting gallery.

Lucy, George, Albert, and me each took a corridor. Stealthily, I eased along the aisle, staying close to the bales, pausing at each corner and clearing the way before moving on, and always searching the catwalks above my head.

Suddenly, the boom of gunfire filled the warehouse with ear-splitting explosions.

I hit the floor and pressed up against a bale as slugs screamed over my head like angry bees.

When the gunfire dropped off, I jerked upright and thumbed off two quick shots in the general direction of our assailants, not expecting to hit anything.

Somewhere behind me, Lucy screamed.

Without hesitation, I dashed down the aisle in her direction, zigzagging ahead of the whining slugs tearing into the wooden floor at my feet.

One struck my heel. I lurched forward, stumbling headlong in an effort to keep my balance.

Then my head exploded with a thousand stars.

Chapter Nineteen

As strange as it may seem, even while unconscious in an inky blackness, I sensed being thrown into a wagon or cart. The sudden jostling of the careening cart snapped me out of my stupor. My head pounded and my muscles ached. This was getting to be a bad habit.

Then I saw Lucy, as tightly bound as I. Her eyes wide with fear, she could only stare at me.

Their backs to us, Leadbelly and Bighead kneeled in the seat opposite us, heads craned out the window, peering behind the cab. "Don't see nobody yet," said Bighead above the clatter of the cab.

"They're back there, dummy," growled Leadbelly.

Our cab bounced over the cobblestone streets and whipped around corners, slinging Lucy and me from side to side. The buildings swept past in a blur and angry shouts from startled pedestrians echoed down the street after us.

Abruptly, the horses whinnied, and the cab jerked to a halt.

A coarse voice called out. "Hold it there, driver. What the blazes is the hurry? You're going to kill someone driving them horses that way."

"Sorry, officer. Got a sick woman in the back. Trying to get her to a doctor."

A short pause, then with a note of suspicion. "What doctor? I don't know of any sawbones around here." The voice moved from the front of the cab to the side. In my mind's eye, I saw the uniformed policeman taking short, careful steps from in front of the horses.

The driver coughed. "Oh? The lady said a doctor named Wilson lived down the street there. Ain't this Tremont Street?"

Another silence.

The driver continued. "You can ask her if you want."

Leadbelly shucked his six-gun and scrunched down in the seat. Bighead kept the muzzle of his .44 on us. I wanted to shout a warning to the lawman, but the hole in the end of that barrel looked the size of a pie plate.

"Maybe I'll just do that," the lawman replied.

Abruptly, Leadbelly sat up and fired point-blank at the law. "Get outta here," he yelled at the driver as the gunshots echoed down the street.

The cab leaped forward.

Behind us, screams filled the street, bounced off the walls of the buildings, and rolled after us.

Bighead kept his six-gun trained on us while Leadbelly peered out the window at our back trail as we twisted and turned through the city.

Skidding around one corner, the cab pulled up, and a large wooden door at the front of a warehouse slid open. The cab clattered inside, and an identical cab shot outside. The door slammed shut behind us.

A few moments later, the pounding of hooves and the rattle of steel wheels against the cobblestone raced past the door, half a dozen wagons at least, following the decoy cab.

Leadbelly grunted as he sat back in the seat. "Reckon we fooled them this time." Then he saw I was awake. A sneer twisted his thick lips. "Well, well, well. Looky here, Bighead. Mr. Smart Alec decided to wake up."

Bighead leered at me. "Yeah. And I owe him too."

Before I could move, a sledgehammer-sized fist caught me between the eyes.

And the all too familiar darkness flooded back over me.

When I awakened, the floor under me was moving, slowly rocking, back and forth, back and forth. I groaned and rolled over on my back.

Lucy's frail voice came from the darkness. "Jim! Jim! You okay?"

I forced my eyes open and stared into the darkness above me. "I . . . I think so, but either it's night or I'm blind."

"Idiot," she whispered angrily. "This isn't the time for jokes."

"Who's joking?" I muttered, blinking my eyes in an effort to see something, anything except the total blackness enveloping me.

Suddenly, a flicker of light reflected off the ceiling. Just as quickly, it disappeared. At least I wasn't blind. Slowly, my eyes focused, and I could make out the dark outline of a window and a few dim stars beyond.

"Where are we?"

From the darkness at my side, Lucy whispered. "On Bordworther's ship. After Bighead knocked you out, they brought us out here. Bordworther plans on throwing us overboard at sea. Seems like Leadbelly made a big mistake when he took us to the warehouse. Curly and Bordworther were there. Bordworther went crazy. He figured all his plans had been exposed. He ordered Curly and the Knotts to bring us out here and drown us.''

A sail popped as the wind caught it, and the schooner lurched. We were underway. The floor rolled under me as I stared into the darkness, struggling to pull myself together. I had to think clearly. ''What happened to George and Albert?''

''Don't know. I don't know what happened to anyone,'' she replied in a hushed voice. ''All I know is that after Bighead coldcocked you they brought us out here.''

''Here? Where's here?''

''In the bay. I told you. We're on Bordworther's schooner. Once they get to sea, they'll throw us overboard. Then there'll be no one to connect them with the counterfeiting.''

I lay silent, feeling the ropes cutting into my wrists, remembering the warnings of the old gambler who raised me, wondering if I'd finally gotten myself into that one big mess that I couldn't handle.

Taking a deep breath, I muttered. ''Well, that only leaves us one choice.'' Before Lucy could reply, I added. ''We've got to get out of here.'' That was one of my more profound remarks.

''Scoot around,'' I whispered. ''Back-to-back.'' I sat up and squirmed around so our backs were together. ''Give me your wrists.''

My fingers, thick and clumsy from lack of circulation, fumbled with the knots. They refused to budge. Sweat rolled down my forehead. I cursed.

"Here. Let me try," Lucy said, pulling her hands away. "Give me your wrists."

Suddenly we froze. Overhead, footsteps thudded across the deck, hesitated, then thumped down the companionway and stopped outside the door.

The door creaked open, and the dim glow of candlelight lit Curly Caruthers's leering face. He extended the candle and the glow fell on us. He grunted. "You two caused me a bunch of trouble."

He set the candle on the table and checked our ropes. "Yeah, you mighta caused us some trouble, but you're goin' to pay for it tonight." He rose and grunted with satisfaction. "Yep. In a couple hours, you'll be fish food."

A sudden scuffling of feet overhead and loud shouts jerked him around. "What the. . . . "

Another burst of shouts galvanized him into action. Without a backward glance, Curly rushed from the cabin, slamming the door behind him.

Lucy frowned at me. I shook my head. "Who knows? But, look what he left behind."

Her eyes lit when she spotted the candle.

I struggled to my feet and backed up to the table, holding my wrists apart and lowering the rope to the flame.

Lucy guided me from behind. "Down some, a couple inches."

I winced as the tiny flame licked at my skin.

"To the left, just a little," she whispered.

Chewing on my lip to suppress the pain in my wrist, I held my hands steady.

"There," she breathed. "Right there."

The sharp smell of burning hair and rope stung my nostrils. I clenched my teeth and tried to shut out the pain.

After what seemed like hours, the first strands parted. Then a few more. The smoke grew thicker.

"It's burning," she whispered. "Hold on."

I strained against the ropes, trying to part them with sheer strength.

Suddenly, the rope snapped.

Lucy gave a soft groan. "You did it. You did it. Now, hurry. Untie me."

I ripped the smoldering ropes from my wrists and tossed them to the floor. Then I quickly freed Lucy.

She turned to face me. "Now what?"

"Follow me." I reached for my six-gun, but all my fingers grabbed was air. They'd removed my gun belt. I picked up the candle and headed for a small hatchway leading into the bowels of the schooner. I froze as soon as I entered the hatch.

Kegs of black powder were stacked to the ceiling. A thought struck me. A fire. I handed Lucy the candle. "Hold this while I stick a match in their shoe."

Lucy frowned, but she didn't question me. She took the candle.

I carried a keg of powder into the cabin and knocked out the bung. Quickly, I poured a string of powder along the base of the bulkhead and across the deck to the hatchway.

"Okay," I said, extending my hand. "Give me the candle."

Her eyes widened in alarm. "What about us?"

"What do you mean, what about us?" I nodded to the window. "We swim. Boston can't be more than a mile or so."

Despite the poor light, I could see her face noticeably pale. A sick feeling hit me in the pit of my stomach. "Is there something I need to know?"

She nodded, and in a whisper, admitted, "I . . . I can't swim."

For several seconds, I stared at her in disbelief. Her announcement was the last thing I expected.

A sudden lurch of the schooner snapped me out of my daze.

I set the candle on the table and glanced around the cabin, searching for some kind of solution to our problem. Maybe a bench or the table, anything that would float. I spotted a chair.

That's when the door burst open. "Now, I'll finish what I started. I. . . . '' Curly Caruthers stood stock-still in the doorway, for a moment, unable to believe his eyes. Then they narrowed, glittering like a demon's in the candlelight.

He bared his teeth in a snarl and reached for his six-gun.

In the same motion, I hurled the chair at him and lunged for his knees.

We crashed into the companionway in a tangle of arms and legs. I tried to jump to my feet, but Caruthers grabbed my leg and sunk his teeth into my calf. I yelled and aimed a kick at him but missed and ended up on my back.

He kept gnawing on my calf, and I jabbed my thumb in his eye. He screamed and grabbed my thumb and tried to bend it back to my elbow. I swung at him with my other fist, but he ducked and I fell over him.

Fighting isn't one of my favorite pastimes, but if I'm forced, I will; however, I prefer fighting erect, not in a ball of clawing fingers and biting teeth like we were.

We rolled several feet along the companionway, and then we rolled back, back and forth, back and forth with each yaw of the schooner, scratching, kicking, cursing.

Finally, I managed to climb to my feet and throw a straight right square into Caruthers's forehead. He stumbled back through the hatchway into the cabin, his arms windmilling in an effort to catch his balance.

He slammed into Lucy, knocking her backwards. She crashed through the window and splashed into the sea.

Chapter Twenty

" "Lucy!" I shouted and dashed for the window. "Hold on!"

She was flailing in the dark water. She tried to speak, but seawater poured down her throat. She gagged.

Don't let her drown. Please don't let her drown, I prayed silently as I reached for her, but a numbing pain struck the back of my neck. I sagged to the floor and caught a boot alongside my head.

Through a dim mist, I saw another boot coming. I grabbed it and twisted.

Caruthers grunted and slammed to the floor.

I scrambled to my feet, desperate to reach Lucy, but Caruthers grabbed my leg and pulled me back. A blinding rage swept over me. I had to get to Lucy, and he was stopping me. "No," I screamed, ripping my foot from his grasp.

He tried to stand, but I swung from the floor and

168

smashed my fist into his throat, knocking him back against the table.

The candle flew across the cabin and landed in the black powder I had spread along the base of the bulkhead. A brilliant white flash illuminated the cabin. For a moment, Curly and me stood frozen like statues, gaping at the hissing flame that raced along the wall.

He yelped and dashed for the door while I spun and dove through the window. In the few seconds before I hit the water, I looked for Lucy, but the darkness covered everything. I couldn't spot her.

The schooner exploded while I was underwater. The shock jarred me. Luckily, the kegs exploded above water, not under. Had that happened, my eardrums would have been blown out, killing me almost instantly.

As it was, I struggled to the firelit surface and searched the sea for Lucy, but she was nowhere to be seen.

The heat grew intense, forcing me to move away from the burning schooner.

Anguish welled up inside of me. Tears clouded my eyes, and a great sadness filled my heart, but I continued swimming first in one direction, and then another, all they while shouting her name.

Just about the time I was ready to give up, I heard a voice. "Jim! Jim! Where are you?"

Lucy's voice cut through the night.

Thrilled, I looked around, trying to spot her. "Here. Over here."

A small dingy emerged from the darkness into the glow of the burning ship. Lucy sat in the bow, paddling toward me.

I couldn't help grinning. That woman sure had a knack for getting out of tough spots. "Here I am," I yelled, waving my arm.

I pulled myself over the gunwale and collapsed on the deck. "I thought you couldn't swim," I managed to gasp out.

Lucy chuckled. "I did too, but I found out that when you're in a hundred feet of water, you can sure surprise yourself. I dog-paddled to the stern and found this dingy tied up. I had just pushed away from the ship when it exploded."

Climbing inside, I seated the oars into the locks and pulled for shore. From the darkness came shouts for help from surviving crew members. "Forget them," I said. "There'll be other boats out here to help. We need to set up some kind of net to see who comes ashore."

The glow of the fire reflected on Lucy's frown. I explained. "A dozen boats'll be out here in a few minutes to pick up the survivors. They'll be landing all along the shore in Boston harbor. If we're not careful, Caruthers and the others will slip through our fingers."

"But, what about the explosion? You don't think it killed them?"

"Can't say. Maybe, but I don't want to take the chance. I don't want Leadbelly or Caruthers or Bordworther to get away."

Within minutes of reaching shore, Lucy had contacted the law and arranged to set up squads of officers along the shoreline of Boston Harbor.

"We'll give it a shot, but it's almost impossible, Miss. Too many miles of shoreline and not enough men," the police chief had said upon hearing her request. "And that don't count the islands."

"I can see what he's talking about," I muttered, standing with Lucy on the dock. "And they might not even come ashore. I wouldn't. If I had the money, I'd buy passage on one of the other ships anchored out in the harbor.''

Throughout the remainder of the night, survivors came ashore, some in boats, a handful swimming, but there was no sign of the Knott brothers or Caruthers or Bordworther.

Mid-morning, the bodies of Bighead and Curly Caruthers washed ashore north of town.

''That leaves Bordworther and Leadbelly,'' I muttered.

Lucy didn't reply.

We watched as the two bodies were loaded into a wagon and covered with a tarp.

''Now what?'' She looked up at me.

I didn't answer for a moment. ''Out there,'' I finally replied. ''There's half a dozen ships anchored. We'll search them.''

We got lucky on the third one. Bordworther was discovered hiding behind bales of tobacco in the hold. That still left Leadbelly. We had no luck on the other three schooners.

Back on shore, Lucy and I went to the police station to meet with Paul Holcombe, the agent replacing Rozell. In addition to Holcombe, we found George and Albert Weems sharing a cell with two drunks and a man who claimed he was the King of Siam.

Miranda was in a cell by herself, still wearing the same blue calico dress, which by now sported ripped seams and dingy lace.

''Can't you get me out of here, Bob . . . I mean, Jim?'' Miranda asked plaintively. ''I ain't done nothing wrong. In fact, I carried William out of the warehouse when he got shot.'' Her face darkened with anger, and she jabbed a meaty finger at the jailer.

"And then them jack-legged idiots tossed me in here."

I glanced at Lucy. She nodded to the jailer and said, "There's no charges against her."

He shrugged. "Whatever you say. What about the other two?" He nodded to George and Albert.

She gave me a sad smile. "They've got to go back to Texas. There's charges they have to answer to."

I spoke up. "But they helped us here."

"And the judge will hear about it. Don't worry. I'm going back to testify for them."

That made me feel better. The Weems were decent people who got sidetracked. Well, they might've helped in the sidetracking, but I figured if someone showed them the right road, they might turn out to be tolerable citizens. Of course, you got to understand, what we called a tolerable citizen in Texas might be considered a public enemy in another state.

As soon as Miranda stepped out of her cell, she hurried to the hospital to see after William, who had taken a slug in the shoulder when we closed in on the warehouse.

After she left, I got all my business straightened out with Paul Holcombe and the Secret Service, which included a check for ten thousand dollars that I carefully deposited in my wallet.

I felt good about everything except Leadbelly. Had he died in the explosion? Or was he alive, just waiting for the time to take his revenge?

"Who knows?" said Lucy. "All we can do is wait and see. Maybe his body will turn up on the beach."

Throughout the ride back to the hotel, the question nagged at me, but I was so exhausted, I pushed it aside and thought only of a clean bed and cool sheets.

Lucy dropped me off at the hotel. "I'll pick you up about six," she said. "The train pulls out at midnight. That'll give us time for a good dinner before we pick up the Weems boys.''

I laid my hand on hers. ''I'm glad you're going back to Texas with us.''

''Me too.'' She smiled. ''Me too.''

I hit the bed, nearly passing out from exhaustion.

I awakened at five, dressed, had a drink in the bar downstairs, and walked onto the sidewalk exactly at six o'clock. I felt naked as a newborn without my six-gun. I glanced around for a gun shop, anxious to feel the comforting weight of a hogleg on my hip. The only gunsmith on the block was closed. I shrugged. Tomorrow would be soon enough.

Five minutes later, a cab pulled up and the ancient driver looked down at me. He studied my head, which, despite a hat, was obviously bald. ''You Jim Wells?'' His voice was a cackle.

''Yep. That's me.''

He handed me an envelope. ''This here's for you.''

With a frown, I took the envelope and tore it open. My blood ran cold as I read it.

Wells,
I got your lady friend here to keep me company
until you get here. Get in the cab and don't send
for no help. If you don't follow my orders, I'll
carve this purty young woman up like fish bait.
                                            Campbell Knott

Chapter Twenty-one

Leadbelly!

I glared at the old driver. "You read this?" I held up the note.

He cackled. "Can't read, mister. Never seen no sense in learnin'. But, I know you need a ride somewhere. Feller what give me the letter told me so."

I clenched and unclenched my fists. Instinctively, I dropped my hand to my six-gun, but my side was bare. I didn't have much choice. "Where we going?"

The old man pointed a bony finger to the south. "Outside of town is a horse hitched to a tree. Directions is tied to the saddle."

For another second, I hesitated. "Okay. Let's go." I climbed into the cab, trying to sort my thoughts. I didn't have time to get help. So, that meant I was in this all by my lonesome.

The cab rattled over the brick and cobblestone

streets, reaching the outskirts at dusk. On a far hill, a white horse grazed beneath a small oak a short distance off the road.

"Here we is," said the driver, pulling off the road. "Yonder's your horse."

Without a backward glance, I strode across the meadow to the grazing pony. Just as the driver had said, a note was tied to the saddle horn. *Ride south!*

I frowned. That's it? That's all there is? I reread the two-word note as if a cryptic message were couched within the two words. Even a third reading could not change the obvious intent.

Leadbelly wanted me to ride south.

"Now, that's not too hard to understand, is it, Wells?" I chastised my own slow thinking.

So, I mounted and rode south.

The sun set behind the hills to the west, and an eerie darkness settled over the rolling countryside, smothering the road ahead with shadows. The narrow road skirted several ponds, a large swamp, and three or four narrow rivers. I had the feeling the road ascended, but I couldn't be sure.

What did Leadbelly have in mind?

"What do you think, stupid?" I muttered. He was going to kill us, that's what he was going to do. I laid my hand on my hip, wishing now I had taken time to find a shop and buy a six-gun.

The waning moon eased over the horizon. Once or twice, I glimpsed the silver sea far to the east. In the distance, an owl hooted, a rabbit squealed.

Suddenly, a gunshot rang out and tore up a chunk of dirt just in front of my horse. The animal reared and pawed at the darkening sky.

"Whoa, boy, whoa." I tightened the reins, pulling the animal back to me. "Easy, easy."

"Wells! That you?"

My pony pranced nervously. "Yeah. What do you want?"

"I'll ask the questions," he shot back. "Understand?" The voice came from a thick copse of undergrowth.

I paused. "Yeah."

"Good. Now climb down off that horse and walk in my direction."

"I can't see you."

"Don't worry about that. You'll see me when you need to."

I did as he said, crossing a small meadow and approaching the thicket. As I grew nearer, a shadowy figure stepped from behind the trunk of a spreading oak.

"Keep coming," growled Leadbelly. "Tie your pony to one of them bushes."

"Okay. Now what?"

"Keep coming."

As I drew closer, I tensed my muscles, hoping for any opportunity to jump him.

"That's far enough. Now, turn around and keep your hands high."

A cold finality settled over me. So this was how I was going to die, I thought to myself. Out in the middle of nowhere, where no one will ever find me.

Steely resolve coursed through my veins. If that's what Leadbelly had in mind, I wasn't about to make it easy for him. I bunched my muscles, ready to leap. I crossed my fingers that I could dodge the slug or that it hit nothing vital until I could get my hands on him.

His next words stayed me. "I'd pay a purty penny to blow your head off, but I need you alive. Now do what I say and turn around."

The tension drained from me, and my muscles went

limp. I turned around as he ordered and stared at Boston lighting the distant horizon like a glittering string. "Where's Lucy?"

Leadbelly grunted. "Alive. For now. Now, shut up."

Behind me came a scraping sound, then the unmistakable tinkle of metal against glass.

Moments later, the glow of a lantern pushed back the night.

"Okay. Turn around and pick up the lantern."

I did as he said.

"Now, straight ahead. To the right of that large beech is a trail. Walk nice and slow. No tricks, or I'll forget I need you."

The light gray bark of the ancient beech tree stood out like a ghost. Overhead, its papery leaves rustled in the breeze like the sound of crumpling paper.

Past the beech, the trail curved to the left and cut into the side of a steep hill. Beyond the hill, a craggy gorge beckoned, the bottom of which disappeared into the shadows far below. The trail narrowed, and I had to place one foot directly in front of the other to keep from slipping off the edge.

The trail curled around a sheer drop-off and ended abruptly at the dark mouth of a cave. I pulled up.

"Inside," Leadbelly growled, jabbing me in the back with the barrel of his six-gun.

I stumbled forward, and the glow of the lantern fell across Lucy, her eyes wide with fear. She struggled against the ropes binding her and tried to speak through the gag tied over her mouth.

Relief washed over me. I set the lantern on the ground and quickly knelt by her side. "Lucy. You okay?" I tore off the gag.

She sucked in a large breath of air and nodded.

"Yeah. I'm fine." Her face was drawn, and dark circles outlined her eyes.

"Awright. Back away from her, Wells. We got business to settle."

Reluctantly, I stepped back and turned to face Leadbelly. He wore a strange grin on his face, reminding me of the crooked grin I once saw on a rabid dog just before he was shot and killed. Leadbelly gripped his six-gun so tightly that his hand shook. Like I told you earlier, I'm no genius, but it didn't take a scholar to see that Leadbelly was wound tighter'n a new clock.

I kept my voice low, unthreatening. "What do you want from me?"

He chuckled. "Bordworther. I want Bordworther." He gestured at Lucy with the muzzle of his six-gun. "Him for her."

"No, Jim. Don't do it," Lucy screamed.

"Shut up, you." Leadbelly erupted and raised the six-gun to whip her across the face.

I took a fast step forward. "Hold it, Leadbelly."

Instantly, he dropped his hand and poked the barrel in my belly. An insane glitter lit his eyes. "One more step, Wells. Please. That's all I ask. One more step."

I froze. He was ready to snap. I kept my eyes on his. He could be pushed just so far. But I needed time, time to find a way to get past that six-gun. "What about Bordworther? If you kill me, what do you do then?"

The nervous, jittery expression on his face was replaced with a calm thoughtfulness. "You can wait." He gave me a light jab in the belly with the six-gun. "Git back against the wall."

"Okay. Just take it easy with that hogleg. I don't care about you or Bordworther. Just tell me what you want."

Lucy squirmed. I shot her a warning glance, then cut my eyes to Leadbelly's feet. She nodded, and slowly, without drawing his attention, drew her knees up.

"Of course, I don't know what good Bordworther will do you or anyone else. Not now," I added.

Leadbelly frowned, his rugged face a canyon of wrinkles. "What are you talking about?"

With a nonchalant shrug, I said. "Bordworther's dead. Hung himself in his cell."

Leadbelly's mouth dropped open.

"That's right. Heard about it just before the cab picked me up with your note." I waited, my eyes fixed on the six-gun. He was half a dozen steps away, far enough to put six slugs in me before I could reach him.

"You're lying."

"No." I took a shot in the dark. "And if it's the money you're after, the police have it."

His face darkened in anger, and his clenched teeth ground in fury. He closed his eyes and turned his face to the ceiling of the cave.

I gave Lucy a quick nod.

She lashed out with her feet, slamming Leadbelly's ankles from under him.

He shouted and tried to swing his six-gun around as he fell. I pounced on him like a bobcat on a mouse, except this mouse was bigger than the bobcat. But I caught him by surprise.

Seizing his gun hand with both of mine, I slammed it against the rocky floor. The six-gun went spinning across the cave.

With the roar of an enraged lion, Leadbelly threw me off and lumbered to his feet. "I'll rip you to pieces, you. . . . "

I didn't have the bulk of Leadbelly, but I was faster.

My fist cut off his cry. I followed up with a left and right cross, whipping his head back and sending him reeling into the wall of the cave.

"Not like that you won't," I taunted him. "You couldn't rip anything to pieces, you overgrown hulk of worthless horseflesh."

Enraged, he charged me, swinging his barrel-sized arms like clubs and screaming at the top of his lungs like a madman. I met him in the middle of the cave. He was overpowering, driving me back against the wall, battering at my arms and head.

I slashed out with a right, catching him on the bridge of the nose. I felt the nose give, and blood squirted down his chin and onto his chest.

A knobbly fist appeared out of nowhere. It caught me in the middle of the forehead and slammed my head against the rocky wall. Stars exploded.

But, I fought back, standing toe-to-toe, hooking lefts and rights, slamming overhands, throwing uppercuts. I landed several blows, but he landed more, and heavier. Slowly, he battered me backwards.

From somewhere deep in the mist threatening to swallow me, I heard Lucy scream, her high-pitched shriek cutting through Leadbelly's roaring.

I thought of Larimer H. Harrison, the gambler who raised me, of Lucy, and yes, of the Weems. I had a lot to live for, a long life ahead, and it was all in my hands.

I reached deep inside and hauled myself up for one last effort.

Leadbelly had me by the shirt and was pounding me against the wall like a rag doll. With a mighty shout, I slammed both my arms up into his, knocking them over his head. Before he could react, I threw four pile-driving fists into his face.

My lungs burned, and I felt my strength quickly

fading. Two more times I hit him, one, a right cross to his cheekbone, splitting the skin under his left eye, and the second, a left hook I threw from the ground. It snapped his chin up and spun him around.

He stumbled and fell headlong into the lantern, smashing it under his bulk.

Flames leaped up, engulfed him, devoured him.

Before I could reach the large man to extinguish the flames, Leadbelly jumped to his feet and, screaming in terror, raced from the cave in a ball of flame.

I shouted. "The ledge. Leadbelly, the led ... "

Too late. The ball of flame shot out of the cave and suddenly disappeared over the ledge. The screams continued, for hours it seemed, but in reality, only seconds.

For a moment, I remained frozen, staring into the darkness where he had disappeared. I stumbled to the edge of the drop-off and stared down at the burning flames deep in the gorge. Leadbelly was dead.

I turned back to Lucy. Slowly, I freed her, my fingers barely functioning.

When her arms were free, she threw them about my neck, and I felt something wet on my cheeks. I gasped out, "You ... You're not hurt, are you?"

"No," she whispered, her face buried in my neck.

"Then ... Then why are you crying?" Another one of my profound questions.

I felt her giggle. "If you don't know ... ," she whispered. Then she kissed me.

Well, that perked me right up. In all my twenty-eight or twenty-nine years, I'd never truly kissed a girl, and suddenly, I discovered what I'd been missing.

I forgot all about my aches and pains, my bruised ribs, the gash on the back of my head where Leadbelly had slammed me into the wall. That kiss was some kind of medicine, I told myself. And I liked it.

The next evening, we settled down on the train for Texas, Lucy, me, George, and Albert. We'd arranged to pick Lorenzo up in Jersey City.

The three brothers would have to stand trial, but there was no killings against them, and they had helped us break the ring of counterfeiters. Paul Holcombe, Rozell's replacement, promised to speak for them at their trial.

Miranda remained in Boston with William.

I had a check for ten thousand dollars in my wallet, a dream of a ranch on the Colorado River in the prettiest section of God's country, but most of all, I had Lucy at my side.